An E

The Baltimore Clan

Tia Therese Mayo

All rights reserved by Tia Therese Mayo.

This book is dedicated to Selah Mo'nae Victor...a beautiful angel.

Table of Contents

Blue Chapter 1 1

Tristan Chapter 2 7

Blue Chapter 3 12

Tristan Chapter 4 19

Blue Chapter 5 24

Tristan Chapter 6 29

Blue Chapter 7 35

Tristan Chapter 8 40

Blue Chapter 9 46

Tristan Chapter 10 51

Blue Chapter 11 56

Tristan Chapter 12 62

Blue Chapter 13 67

Tristan Chapter 14 70

Blue Chapter 15 73

Tristan Chapter 16 82

Blue Chapter 17 87

Tristan Chapter 18 93

Blue Chapter 19 98

Tristan Chapter 20 103

Blue Chapter 21 107

Tristan Chapter 22 113

Blue Chapter 23 116

Tristan Chapter 24 .... *119*

Blue Chapter 25 .... *123*

Tristan Chapter 26 .... *126*

Blue Chapter 27 .... *130*

Tristan Chapter 28 ....*135*

Blue Chapter 29 .... *141*

Tristan Chapter 30 .... *147*

Blue Chapter 31 .... *152*

Tristan Chapter 32 .... *158*

Blue Chapter 33 .... *165*

Tristan Chapter 34 .... *170*

Blue Chapter 35 .... *173*

Tristan Chapter 36 .... *179*

Blue Chapter 37 .... *184*

Tristan Chapter 38 .... *188*

Blue Chapter 39 .... *191*

Tristan Chapter 40 .... *195*

Blue Chapter 41 .... *201*

Tristan Chapter 42 ....*205*

Blue Chapter 43 .... *209*

Blue Chapter 44 .... *213*

Tristan Epilogue Chapter 45 .... *218*

BLUE CHAPTER 1

"Have a productive day in school. Oh, and don't forget to be here at six o'clock sharp for dinner," My mom's voice rang out.

"Yes ma'am," I yelled back on my way out the door.

"Love you," She yelled down the hall but I had already closed the door.

Waking up in a cold sweat, I was having the same dream or rather nightmare that I have periodically. I keep dreaming about the last encounter I had with my mom while I was still a human. The fact that I was rushing out and I never said 'I love you too' still gets to me. I was dragged and attacked in a Baltimore alleyway not far from my home. I remember I was being followed by things that were even scarier than the dark alley itself. The gloomy day changed my life forever.

I remember the smell of my assailant like it was just yesterday and not forty-nine years ago. Even though, only one guy attacked me, I can remember there were a few of them. A tall dark emancipated looking one smelled of Gucci black cologne with a mix of an indescribable musk. I remember his cold hands that had so much strength behind them. He came up from behind me and grabbed my jaw, clinched it so tight I thought my teeth would rupture through my cheeks. I immediately felt enraged for giving anyone the opportunity to sneak up on me. I am usually abnormally aware of my surroundings and even though I knew they were there, I couldn't remember when I allowed this one to get so close to me. *He had to have ran* I thought. But even if he did, that would make him insanely fast. Because at that point I was still naïve to the world. It was a very dreary day and my mom told me countless times not to walk through the alleys to get to my classes at the college I attended. I took her advice with a grain of salt, thinking the odds of someone bothering me were slim.

I walked this alley a few times every week for over a year. I was an accountant major. I was, well I am amazing with numbers. I knew that attending college and excelling the way that I had, made my mom really proud. I already had a few clients that I ran small books for as an accountant. I had a great buzz around me already and I was getting phone calls from new prospective clients for after I graduate.

My attacker ripped my turtle neck, exposing my bra and popping my pearl necklace. He had me in his grip with my back against his hard chest, that's when fear tried to creep in. I couldn't allow that. I would not be a screaming victim. I fought as hard as I could, and that's saying a lot considering I've been taking karate since I was three years old. He was still behind me, I kicked him as hard as I could in his shins, and he didn't budge. He grabbed my face harder and got very close to my neck, and deeply inhaled.

"You're a damn creep!" I gritted my teeth and I still did not scream because that is what a lot of attackers get off on.

"It's easier if you did not try to fight this," he said in a very monotone voice.

I wasn't going to give him the satisfaction. But my head was racing with thoughts. Fear. Why was this guy so cold? And what did he want with me? His cologne and musky scent mixed with the smell of the rotting garbage in the alley was too much. It was nauseating. I suddenly felt a sharp pain on my neck. I tried kicking again with no luck. Something was off with this guy. I later found out he was a vampire recruiter of sorts. I tried to punch him but the angle I was in only allowed very small movements of my arms, so I wasn't doing any damage. I took a second to breathe deep and gathered my thoughts, I could feel myself getting weak from being held in the position so long. I decided screaming for help might actually be my only chance. Once I let out a shrill, with everything I had left in me, he moved his hand to my mouth to try and cover it. I somehow got my teeth around his hand and bit down as hard as I could. I felt my face get released. I started running away but my body betrayed me and I went down into the disgusting dirty alley. My last thoughts before passing out were of my mother and how disappointed and saddened she would be when she found my body. I blacked out. This was my last day as a human, but my mom never found a body.

That was forty-nine years ago and so much has changed but I still miss my mom like it was yesterday. The pain it caused her after my so-called death will haunt me until I die, again. The only thing that helps me cope is knowing that she died in peace. A year ago, while my mom was on her death bed, I broke all the vamp rules and visited her in hospice. Cancer sucks. A human knowing about our kind could be punishable by death or the human must join the clan and become an enlightened human but none of that mattered because I knew my mom barely had any time left on this earth. My heightened sense of smell actually got a whiff of the decay of rotting flesh in her body. How awful was this? A lady gives her entire life to the military, dodging all kinds of bullets and bombs that came her way only to come home and be slowly killed by cancer. My fist balled up in anger. I knew I owed her a peaceful death by letting her know her only child was okay. After reassuring her and letting her know I was doing well, she smiled. Even though she was slowly slipping away, my mom still had the most beautiful smile in the world.

"I knew it baby. I kept telling everyone if K'ly was dead I would have felt her soul leave, I would feel as if there were a piece of my heart that went missing, but I never felt any of that," She croaked out.

"I love you mom," I whispered.

"I'm not going to question you and ask you why you look exactly as you did forty-nine years ago when you last walked out my door. Or what has happened to your eyes." My eyes were now as blue as the ocean but when I left that day, they were a pretty golden brown. "I'm just going to sit here and enjoy your company Ly. Whatever you are doing baby, you better still be the leader I raised you to be. You better still open up your mouth when something doesn't sit well with you. You don't have to try hard to lead because you are a natural born leader, that was your gift in life." She began to cough a little.

"You never have to be the loudest in the room. Your presence is known as soon as you walk into the room. Always remember that. Do me a favor and grab my purse." I went over to the small closet and grabbed the purse that was hanging on the door. It was a vintage Prada. It was so light due to her OCD not allowing her to overload it with stuff like some women. She rummaged through it swiftly with her tired hands. Whatever she was looking for, she knew exactly where it would be.

"I need you to take this. It belongs to you." She handed me an old musty book. It looked so ancient. I opened it but there was nothing but blank red pages. I quickly put the book in my Chanel bag. She coughed a little more. I grabbed her hand and nodded; my eyes watered a little. I could tell this was the end.

"No tears Ly," she told me. I straightened up. My mom was the toughest person I knew and she was very tough on me growing up. I used to think she wished she had a son but I later realized she just wanted me to be just as tough as any man so that I would never have to depend on one.

"But what is this?" I asked a little louder than a whisper.

"It belonged to your father. I don't know any details, but guessing by your eyes and the fact that you haven't aged, I know I completed my life's mission." She breathed in and smiled a little.

"K'ly"

"Yes mom?"

"I'm at peace now." She assured. My beautiful mother then began to cough and fit. I gave her some water, her alarms started going off.

"I love you." She croaked out.

"I love you too." I wiped her gray hair from her forehead and took in how beautifully she had aged. Then she was gone. I felt her leave. I felt her soul smile at me as it rose out of her body and continued on a journey, not of this earth. I had so many questions that I felt I'd never get the answers to.

TRISTAN CHAPTER 2

I was stuck inside of my own mind again. I was at a party with some of my boys, Andre and Terrell. Andre was a warlock and Terrell was a vampire like myself. I just couldn't get into the party mood. I guess I am getting older. I just did not enjoy the party scene like I used to. We were at our usual V.I.P booth taking shots and flirting with Aubrey, our waitress for the night. We were at the hottest club for supernaturals on the west coast and here I was reminiscing about my mom, well trying to. I couldn't remember what exactly she looked like anymore and I only knew her first name. I know I have been a vampire for many years but I can only remember the last few and I find it odd that I can't remember what my own mom looked like or find any photos. When I tried to remember my head started to hurt.

"You good?" Andre asked.

"Yea I'm fine, I think ima head in early tonight though," I told him

"Seriously, have you not noticed the witches at the bar giving us looks all night? I just sent over a three hundred dollar bottle of champagne you can't leave now bro," Andre pleaded.

"He's probably still thinking about Blue, you know she had him whipped," Yelled Terrell over the music. They laughed.

"I haven't seen or talked to her in months, this is not about her." But honestly, it kinda was. Ever since I was with Blue no other woman has been as satisfying and its so frustrating. It didn't make sense. Everyone knew me as Tristan the womanizer. I always enjoyed the ladies and they have always enjoyed me. How did I get like this? Lately, I have been more and more interested in the why. I wanna say I had a regular upbringing, a good mom, a nice home and all that but I'm having trouble really focusing on any particular memory. Weird. The three pretty witches from the bar came over and tore me from my thoughts. They were so giddy and giggly like young college girls. One pounced right on my lap.

"Hello red head," she purred, rubbing her hands all on my chest. She was pretty and had a nice body but was really throwing herself at me. She had on a glitter looking bra and fuzzy skirt, there was nothing to be left to the imagination with this one. I removed her hand from my chest and placed it in her lap.

"Hello to you." I was looking at her in her eyes.

"There is enough room here at the booth for you to sit right here." I patted the empty seat beside me. With a huff and pouty lips, she got off my lap and sat beside me. When did I become this guy?

"What's your name? What do you do?" I asked.

"I'm Crystal and I work at the gap." She was back to rubbing me down again. I guess I wasn't giving her the attention she wanted because she got all pouty again.

"I did not spend a hundred dollars on this white lily just to come over here and talk about work." She shook some small powder in a tiny package in her fingers.

"I'm going to the lady's room," she said and stormed off. *What the hell is white lily?* I thought. I looked around. Her friends were really enjoying my guys. They were all kissing and feeling on each other. Andre got his lips free for just a second to tell me to relax and that I wasn't being myself. Truth is I was ready to go without pouty mouth, but for some reason when she returned, I asked if she wanted to dance. She got super happy.

"I thought you would never ask." She beamed.

After a few shots of Patron, I was totally back in my zone, with everything but my mother on my mind. She wasn't the best dancer but I made it work. After a good while, I decided I was ready to leave. If my boys hadn't made good impressions on the ladies they were with by now, then they should just give up. I knew fuzzy skirt (or Crystal) would be ecstatic to leave here with me and I was right.

I drove my bike here. So, I gave her my only helmet. We stopped at a convenience store outside of my community, called the Caves, to grab some snacks. (Yes, some vampires still enjoy snacks). I was already on my bike waiting for her to come outside when I heard screams.

What the hell is going on? I thought to myself. I looked up just in time to see Crystal throw a fireball at the store clerk who luckily dodged it. I run in and grab her and throw her on my bike. I look back and saw a few store employees trying to put out the fire. It looked like no one was hurt. I will have to straighten this all out tomorrow. Luckily, the workers were all enlightened humans or else we would be in an even bigger mess.

"What the hell were you thinking?" I demanded once we were inside my apartment. She looked up and down, then looked around my place and smiled.

"Why the hell should I have to pay humans for anything. They are lucky us witches even tolerate them at all. They are beneath us," She said.

"What are you talking about? They are good people and I live here." I seethed. She did not even respond. Something was off with this one. Why do I always end up with the crazy females? *I need to learn more about this white lily drug.* I thought to myself.

BLUE CHAPTER 3

That last conversation I had with my mom was something she told me every day; that I was born to lead. Her unforgettable words were a driving force to me becoming clan leader. The thought of running this clan had been on my mind for a while but it took some time for me to actually decide that's what I wanted to do. There were so many changes here at the Roses that I felt needed to be made. The first one would be to ban unwilling vampire recruiting. There were enough vampires already.

You'd think after what happened to me in that alley that I'd be fed up and disgusted with all the crime going on here. Not only did regular everyday crime happen often but now I knew supernatural crime was happening as well. The crime rate was high here, everyone knew that, and I decided the last thing the city needed was vampires contributing even more to that. Especially considering many of us had family here one way or another. This was the final push for me to run the United States east clan. Baltimore was one of those places where there were always whispers that there were things living amongst us other than just humans. I will admit that I personally never gave it much thought unlike many of my old friends. I even remember my mother warning me as a child that sometimes things would happen here that were hard to explain. After being turned I often wonder if my mom knew there were vampires and witches here in the shadows?

Surge, a former militant, had been by my side since I first decided I would fight for the USE (United States east coast clan) to become clan leader and overthrow King. King's real name was John before he became the clan leader, but he felt the name King was more befitting. What an arrogant vamp he was. He had been clan leader since before I arrived here. Many in the clan told me they disliked him and definitely did not trust him. No one really remembers how he came to be clan leader in the first place and that's where the distrust started. He enjoyed bringing young human girls into our community called the Roses. Our true identity was kept a secret for our safety and peace. We basically lived next door to humans but with our building by the Baltimore National Harbor being cloaked it just seemed like a luxury apartment building. So what King was doing to the human girls was extremely idiotic and careless and most importantly sick. He made my blood boil and my skin crawl. I couldn't bear the thought of what he was doing with the young girls and apparently, I wasn't alone in my disgust. The only reason half of us were here was because of him and his unnecessary recruiting. The rumor is he was trying to create as many vamps as he could just in case there was ever a war amongst the clans. But did he really think we would fight for him?

My best friend Reece was the second person I told that I was going to take him down. I made her promise not to say a word but of course, she just had to tell her fiancé Micah. We later found out there were many others who wanted to join just to take him out and would stand beside me.

If Surge was my right hand, then Micah was left. He was a tall dark, long legged man with the temper of a bull, and memory like an elephant. I was a little bothered by Reece breaking her promise of keeping my secret to herself. I am woman enough to admit that Micah alongside Surge and I, was how we became the powerful trio we are today. It was no easy feat defeating King. He was cold and ruthless, and worse of all he was centuries older than I was, which gave him the advantage of strength. His downfall however was his addiction to women, and not having anyone he could trust. The three of us made a plan and once we decided to kick in King's door that night, we knew there was no turning back. Most of his guards were just like him when it came to women. So, Reece used her womanly curves and power that all of us women have to distract the main guard. Her long flowing locs, Carmel complexion and hazel eyes were more than enough to get a man's attention. Micah was not happy with this plan but he was out voted. Once she got the main guard's attention, she cornered him and placed him under a sleeping spell. My best friend is a powerful witch who has barely even tapped into her potential. Do not make Reece mad.

We knew King would be in bed with his many human slaves. He was so predictable we knew where he was going to be, what he was going to be doing and we also knew which of his guards despised him; which were plentiful because he just wasn't a nice person. So, we met up with one of his guards prior and he agreed to drug a few of the other guards an hour before our planned attack. Weeks before that I met up with a few of his lower ranking guards that also despised him and they agreed to join our side. You're probably wondering why would I trust the guards, well let's just say I had a gut feeling.

That entire night seemed to happen in a blur. We kicked in his door; Surge was to my left Micah on my right. They took down the only two guards who did not take the sleeping spell or switch sides in a quick scuffle. They then stood back because this was my fight. Clan law stated that the person who wanted to become leader must fight the current leader. Primitive, I know. King stood a whole foot above me. Wiping crust from his eyes he laughed.

"Your joking, right?" I watched the women that were in his bed scramble to get their things and get into a corner for safety. He looked at Micah then Surge.

"You guys are serious? Y'all gonna let this little bitch get y'all killed?" He asked. Micah and Surge were silent. He didn't even deserve a response.

"Well so be it," He retorted. I didn't allow him to even take a swing at me. I punched him as hard as I could in the gut since people are always expecting a swing for the face first. While he was bent over from the blow, Surge threw a machete at me. It was slicing through the air at an incredible speed, but Surge and I practiced this throw for years when he trained me. One second off and I would lose my entire hand. I caught it perfectly and in one swift motion, I released King of his duties by removing his head. Immediately Micah lit his ass on fire and spit on it. Loyalty was everything to them, they would die for me because they knew I would die for them. We never discussed why they choose to follow me or believe in me but I could never pay them back for it. Besides love can't be bought. So, there is no payback.

Was it a low blow hitting King during what I knew was his moment of weakness? I would say it was but I don't regret a minute of it. It was not only necessary but also a little exhilarating. See this wasn't our first time meeting or exchanging words. Our first run-in was in a cute little café called Silver Queen Cafe in the Hamilton area years ago, even though I had been in this clan for over thirty years at that point. I was following my hostess to my seat when I noticed him. He was dining with about four women. I wasn't sure if they were groupies or slaves. One was a vamp but the ones with their heads down and mouths shut were humans. I stood staring at all of them for a while. The hostess didn't notice and kept walking.

"Miss, will this table work for you?" She questioned.

"Sure."

I was supposed to be meeting Surge here for a business meeting but he was running late. I ordered my mimosa, and tried to get my thoughts off of King and the humans. It was a struggle but once I got into my phone and read my emails, I quickly got bombarded with business. The club Surge and I owned was in desperate need of more hosts. The waiter came to my table.

"Miss, the gentlemen over there sent this over." She nodded her head in the direction of King. It was a bottle of wine. The cheapest bottle they carry, I might add. Vampires especially old vampires have no shortage of money so the cheap wine was definitely an insult.

"I would like to send it back," I told her.

"Well, it's already paid for." She assured looking down at her feet. I could tell the waiter was scared of King.

"Okay," I said. I took the bottle from her and continued drinking my mimosa. I'll just give it to the homeless man outside. I decided I couldn't wait any longer for Surge so I paid my tab and gathered my things. As I was walking past King's table he said,

"Wow no thank you or nothing? You really need to be taught some manners." He said as he sneered. Ugh, I felt so icky as his eyes practically undressed me. A pig. He allowed his fangs to slowly come down, which was a big no no when we were out at a human establishment. I leaned onto his table and for the first time the humans looked up. I noticed bruising around their necks but I hid my anger well and I kept my voice low.

"Only cowards hurt women. Your time will come and I hope I knock that disgusting smile off your face." I noticed one of the women nodded in approval but most were high as hell off of something. He didn't handle strong women well. King stood up angrily and very clumsy-like, spilling a drink all over himself in the process. One human barely giggled and he gave her a look that would scare even the toughest of people. I was almost out the door by now.

"You must have lost your damn mind! Your braids must be too tight. Nobody talks to King like that you big butt cunt. King demands respect!" He yelled behind me. Mission accomplished, I had him rattled. Thinking back on it all, I'm so glad I chopped his head off. I just wish he would have suffered more.

TRISTAN CHAPTER 4

After that rendezvous with the crazy witch last night, I'm almost happy to be getting ready for meetings. The keyword here is almost. Unfortunately for me, I have to attend every meeting and I really disliked them. But duty calls since I was a general, second in command only behind Camilla herself. Once I arrived at the multipurpose building, I sat down in my normal seat beside her. I had to be here and listen to the complaints of our clan as well as the pleas from witches, warlocks, and sometimes enlightened humans. They all came periodically to plea with Camilla about joining the Cali clan (United States West coast clan). Today was no different and first up was a witch named Lucy. When it came to anyone that wasn't a vampire, she never even lifted her eyes to acknowledge them. After they finished talking, she always said the same thing.

"Cali clan is no place for any kind except our own kind. I must always keep my clan safe even if that means keeping you all out. Seek out USE, I hear she is desperate for more…people." She was examining her manicure the entire time treating Lucy like she wasn't even worth the conversation.

She was talking about Blue of course. The vampire whose eyes were blue like the waters in Porto Katsiki of Greece. They poured right into your soul. I've never met a woman with as strong a presence as Blue, not even Camilla demanded attention so effortlessly. Blue's strength came from her compassion and empathy for others. Camilla's came from fear. Fear of being murdered by her own clan members as her father was. And there I was doing it again. Comparing Blue to Camilla, but honestly, there was no comparison because from the moment I laid eyes on Blue, I felt something deep in my chest began to stir. A sensation I've never felt before.

It's hard to explain but I felt it and when our eyes met, I immediately thought *she had to be mine!* It was weird to say because I've never been a one-woman guy or even a romantic guy. Women always flocked to me. For as long as I could remember, I never had to try hard to get a woman. If I'm being completely honest with myself, I was definitely a dog but that was years ago. I would like to believe that I have calmed down …somewhat. Besides after I looked into Blue's eyes, I knew I no longer wanted to be the dog, or a lover boy. I wanted to be a man. I wanted to be her man, but her stubborn ass wouldn't let me.

Five years ago, Camilla wasn't in charge of Cali clan yet. Mr. Brinks, Camilla's dad was still in power. Blue and Mr. Brinks had a meeting scheduled to discuss traveling witches safe passage through both US clans. This is when I first laid eyes on Blue. She pulled up at the multipurpose building in a large new Tahoe followed by two other black SUVs. I was rushing past to get into the building just as her driver was opening her door. I was stopped dead in my tracks. I just stood there and stared at her for a second.

"Keep your eyes on your business boy." A very large older guy in a tight suit warned me as he stood beside her truck with his huge arms folded in front of him. He looked like a huge robocop. We stood eyeing each other and I wasn't in the least bit intimidated. Clearly, this guy doesn't know who I am.

"Surge let's go. You know how I feel about punctuality." Her voice was like velvet. Mr. muscles stood there and waited for her to walk past him.

"Big bald head ass," I murmured under my breath. But I know he heard me. He was itching for me to do anything inappropriate. I wasn't sure if he was her bodyguard or if she was a natural born vampire, he could have been her father. I was a little annoyed with myself for not coming up with anything cunning or slick to say since that's usually my forte. I finally got my shit together and ran up and held the door open for her. She walked with ease in her high heels, and her skirt suit fit like a glove but didn't look too tight. Could have been tailor made but I wouldn't really know.

"I think we are going to the same place," I said with my dazzling smile.

"Unlikely." she looked me up and down. I had on my favorite Levi jeans a snug white tee shirt and fila disruptor II sneakers. I know I don't dress like a general, trust me I hear it all the time from Camilla. I just wasn't into the whole suit and dress shoes thing. Camilla understood I wasn't going to budge once my mind was set. She also knew no one would protect her life as well as I do, no matter what they were wearing. I continued to hold the door and admired Blue's body as she walked past. Her skirt suit was royal blue which complimented her dark brown skin as well as her blue eyes. Her hair was in braids, going straight down her back all the way down to her nice round butt. She was slim thick, very curvy. Perfection. She was so bad.

I entered the meeting and quickly sat down to the right of Mr. Brinks. Blue and Surge took their seats and two guards remained standing behind her. My phone rang.

"What's up?" I asked. The voice on the other end replied, "We need you to go to Section II, Bruce and the new guy are going at it." I told Mr. Briggs and Camilla I'd have to sit this meeting out. I motioned for another guard to take my seat beside our clan leader. We had a new natural born vampire named Lolli who just joined us here at the caves. He was super sneaky and I did not trust him. I mean who leaves a well-known clan in a very good position to come here and become a nobody?

"I got it." Hanging up I was slightly disappointed for the first time that I would be missing the meeting. Leaving out of the building I proceeded to my Kawasaki. Living up here in the mountains in Cali was beautiful. I definitely believe we had the most beautiful living settings of all the clans that I've visited. The Cali clan resides in caves in the mountains that consisted of small apartments, studios, villas, and a few penthouses. Each apartment had rooftop skylights that allowed us to look at the beautiful sky day or night but blocked out the sun rays to protect our skin. The sun, contrary to popular belief, does not kill vampires, it does however burn turned vampires when exposed too long. It is extremely uncomfortable for natural born vampires. Natural born vampires have much tougher skin. But we all try and avoid it as much as possible. My motorcycle was perfect for the narrow trails that led from one section of the caves to the next. Most of us that lived here drove bikes, or very small cars because of the convenience. Honestly, I don't know how Blue's huge SUVs even made it up the trails without falling off the side of the mountain. The breeze felt amazing as I zoomed through the narrow tunnels and streets making my way to section II. I think back now on how even back then I could not get the blue-eyed clan leader out of my head. My phone ringing snapped my attention back to the present. It was Camilla. Shit! She sounded pissed. She must have found out about the witch incident last night at the store.

BLUE CHAPTER 5

A hard knock on my door snapped my attention out of my account books. I always enjoyed working on my numbers on a Friday night. My golden retriever Moo Moo began to bark and run toward the door. I looked at my Ring doorbell camera expecting to see one of my guards, but who stood outside my door surprised me. It was Allegra, a rogue vampire that I had one too many encounters with. It was strange seeing her here considering she made it well known that she wanted nothing to do with this clan. She wasn't a part of any clan but had associates in many. Gorgeous as she was (I'm talking Russian supermodel type) she came with drama and problems. She also had this huge fight with Reece a few years back and still had no respect for their relationship. So, she wasn't on my buddy list. Accompanying her was Red, the eldest witch in my clan. Why were they here at this time of the night? I let them in and as soon as I was about to close the door behind me there was another knock on the door. This time it was less of a surprise.

"Blue are you alright?" It was Surge of course. Surge was my second in command, number one security guard and business partner. So, him living directly across the hall from me made sense. He was my right hand guy, the person I trusted most. I opened the door.

"I'm fine Surge go to bed." I stood in my doorway while he tried to peek into my apartment from the doorway. He crossed his huge arms and just stared at me for a second. Then he sighed.

"If I hear anything, I will be right back over here. He began to retreat into his home.

"Come Asmer." His pet Siberian Husky was in the hall playing with Moo moo. After Moo Moo came in, I closed the door behind her. Since I became clan leader, I changed our laws to not only allow pets to live at the Roses, but they live super enriched lives. We have a puppy playroom, a vet on site and a mobile groomer named Tia that services all our pets. Many of us can't have children so why not have man's best friend?

"Hello Allegra, hello Red what is going on?" I asked. Allegra sat down on my stiff sofa while Red remained standing. Allegra was the first to speak up.

"There's a new drug hitting the clubs hard. I'm not sure if it's made it's way here to Baltimore yet but it's already in Europe," She said.

"You came all this way to tell me about a drug? There must be more to the story." I pointed out.

"Well, there is..." She looked at Red.

"I've never seen anything like it and I know drugs. Last night my friend Cassie took the drug and became violent, mercurial, and hostile. She was so unlike herself. The drug affects everyone so differently. At first it was your normal high but then it started to make vampires paranoid of each other. I was fighting with her, trying to get her to calm down and take her home when suddenly three men dressed in gray suits came out of nowhere took her." She tried to fight back tears.

"When I find the people responsible for this, I'm going to crush them. Cassie is the good one she doesn't deserve this!" She blubbered through her thick Russian accent.

"Who gave you the drugs?" I asked

"I am not on a first name basis with every drug dealer I meet." She scowled.

"Well, who took her? Do you know what they could have wanted?" I asked feeling very perplexed. "You and Cassie get into a lot of mess, to be frank. How do I know this isn't just some vampires trying to get revenge on you two for something you may have done?"

She glared at me through red puffy eyes. "The kidnappers were humans. Ugh, why did I even try to come and warn you? I don't know what makes you feel so superior as if you are perfect when you and I both know that isn't true." I knew exactly what she talking about but I kept my face calm. She took a few steps toward me.

"I'm done with this. But just so we are clear if you hear anything about a drug called white lily, don't allow it in your club or in the Roses. Its human made I believe and we can't trust them. See you later Red." She let herself out.

I looked over at Red. Her wise wrinkled face remained the same. I admired her she always looked so calm no matter what.

"What do you make of all this?" I asked her.

"Well, the witch community feels uneasy too. Something is shifty in the air. I downtown having lunch with a witch I have known for years. We took a walk by the harbor and everything was fine. All of sudden she just jumped in the water and drowned." She shook her head. Her eyes smothered with sadness.

"Think about it, have you ever heard of a witch drowning? We literally are all taught from birth how to protect ourselves from water and fire. It was as if she wasn't herself all of a sudden. Like perhaps she was on drugs or something."

"I'm so sorry. Make sure she has a lovely memorial. Spare no expense." She hugged me tightly. I had more questions, but now wasn't the time. She needed time to grieve.

"Please be safe Blue."

"I should have offered Allegra a safe place to stay until all this was figured out," I confessed.

"Don't worry about Allegra. You know she doesn't want to be a part of any clans, she loves the freedom and excitement of being rogue." And with that, she left. I could not go back to my numbers after learning of all this. I need to figure out what was going on and was this all connected?

TRISTAN CHAPTER 6

It was a weekend night and here I was home alone. Maybe my boys are on to something. Maybe I was changing. I mean, I can't even remember the last time I actually stayed in on a weekend. I sat down in my favorite recliner and ordered myself an enlightened human to feed on. Even though I understood where Blue was coming from with her decision to be abstinent from drinking humans, I allowed myself fresh blood every few days or so. It was like ordering a pizza. Here at caves and many other clans, we kept enlightened humans or EHS close in a nearby village. They were all volunteers because they were paid substantially well. There was a knock on the door as soon as I hung up the phone.

I looked through my peephole. It appeared to be a small woman but it was hard to tell because had her head down and covered with a hood. She looked up immediately and it almost looked as if she was staring right at me through the peephole. She had a very young face. What the hell was she doing at my door? She definitely wasn't here to be my food and her eyes were too bold. I decided I wasn't in the mood for this right now. I tiptoed backwards and was almost back to my recliner.

"I know you are in there Tristan. Please let me in, it's not safe for me to be here but I had to meet you and see if all of this was true." She spoke in a hushed tone through the door. *'All of what was true?'* I wondered.

"Okay you have my attention," I said as I began unlocking the door and opening it. "But I promise you will regret it if this is some type of setup." She came inside and took off her hood. I had to blink several times. Her face had so much of an odd familiarity to it.

"Hello, Tristan." She said it like we knew each other for years instead of her being a complete stranger.

"Do I know you? What do you want? And why do you look so familiar?" I asked her, becoming a little impatient by this unannounced guest just standing there staring at me. I circled her trying to read her.

"Where are your manners, Tristan?" She asked with a mischievous smile. She began walking around, looking at my things and running her hands across my furniture.

"Okay I shouldn't have let you in, it's time to go, it's clear you do not want anything." I walked to the door and held it open for her. She came over with lightning speed and slammed it.

"You're no fun, just like dad! But fine I will start talking." She said as she plopped down on my favorite recliner and drank my glass of rum I had just poured for myself.

"Your kind of a brat. Start talking now kid or get out. And why do you look so familiar who are you?" I said her, frustrated with all of this.

"I look familiar because I look like you! We have the same father, Tristan." She was locked onto my face waiting to see my expression I suppose but there wasn't much to see because I wasn't buying it. But the more I stared at her, the more I saw the truth. Her deep set hazel eyes were almost identical to mine. She had the same set of dimples, the same full lower lip. And the natural red hair was undeniable.

"I don't know my father, so how do you know who my father is?" I asked her.

"Okay look I'm not supposed to be here Tristan but I wouldn't be a good sister if I did not come and warn you. Rumor has it that your mother kept you hidden from us. I'm not sure how she did it. But you look like a good guy. Like the type of guy that my world would chew up and spit out. So, your best bet is to stay far far away from the Royals clan." She told me.

"Wait. You want me to believe that I am of royal pureblood?" I chuckled a little. Her face remained the same.

"I shouldn't be here so the least you could do is take this seriously. You are a Royal and my relentless dad has searched up and down the globe for you, only recently has he finally given up." She told me.

"You've wasted your time coming here. I mean come on, if I were a natural vampire, I wouldn't have had to be turned."

"But were you really turned or were you made to believe you were turned? What do you remember of your childhood?" she asked. I was drawing a blank. I actually had little to no memories of anything before I came to caves. She looked at her phone as it began to ring.

"I have to go," she said "but just know this, no one knows you are still alive. Rumor is that my mom, who's a total bitch by the way, threatened to kill you in your sleep if you stayed with us any longer. You are the makings of a drunk night mixed with infidelity. My mom doesn't handle jealousy well. Your mom tried to keep her from finding out but I mean, look at you and your chiseled cheekbones and the red hair." She waved her hand up and down my silhouette and added, "You could be father's twin. So instead, your mom must have stashed you and had your memory erased before she was…" she looked away from me dramatically.

"Before she was what?"

"Um my father claimed that your mother disobeyed him when she took you from our home. They had her…" she ran her finger across her throat.

"What?" I was kinda glad I did not remember who my mom was at this moment.

"Sorry," She answered. She looked anything but empathetic.

"Okay let's say I believe you, answer this. Why are you here? You traveled god knows how far just to tell me all this why?" I demanded. Her red curly hair danced around her as she shook her head.

"Because as long as you keep your distance, I am next in line to run the Royals clan brother. Just look at the proof I've left you. It was taken around the last time you were still with us." And in the blink of an eye before I could even respond she was gone. She was super fast like me, maybe even faster. I was reeling. I noticed a very old folder in the recliner where she was just sitting at. I opened and there was only one thing in it. It was a picture of me, maybe 8 or 9 and I was holding an infant girl. On the back it said Tristan and Tabitha 1941. I continued to stare at the picture in disbelief. A creepy eerie feeling ran through me but a knock on the door snapped me out of my thoughts. It was my EHS. Problem was I had lost my appetite. I sent the human away. When I finally got comfortable in my recliner there was yet another knock on the door. It was Terrell.

"Hey bro! I wasn't expecting you tonight." I gave him a look before letting him. I don't like unexpected visits and this was the second one tonight.

"Sorry for just popping by Tristan but I wanted to warn you. Those witches we were hanging with last weekend were nothing but trouble. It smells like a woman in here, you got company?" He asked sniffing the air.

"No. I don't." I told him, getting even more annoyed. By now he was raiding my fridge looking for a beer.

"What do you mean the witches were trouble?" I said raising my eyebrows.

"Man, that bitch gave me something! I always thought witches could do a spell and keep their shit together." He was livid. I couldn't do anything but laugh. We ended up playing 2k all night and threw back several beers. I'm was so thankful I did not fool around with crazy Crystal.

BLUE CHAPTER 7

Since I was now the ruler of the USE clan, I was responsible for keeping my people safe and unlike most clans, we had an open door policy. Any and all species were welcome in USE. I was responsible for making sure everyone was safe that joined us. I made sure the cloak that kept the Roses safe was never wavering so that the humans couldn't get much further than our front lobby unless invited. I was also responsible for either avoiding war or causing it. There were always a million things resting on my shoulders at once but I managed. Being a woman and being of color didn't always help matters either. I've met so many older male vampires that hated my guts and didn't do much to try to hide it. I have only had a few situations where the disrespect almost crossed the line but each time that happened Surge always stepped in and played the mediator. Seeing as though I was the first female leader of a clan on the east coast, I kinda understood the resentment. But I did not have time to focus on that. I was on my way to my underground nightclub in little Italy that I owned with Surge.

Once I arrived, I sucked in a deep breathe to get a feel for the energy. Tonight, it was felt very positive or at least as positive as it could be considering it was a pasty bar. Kitty's Time used to be a very sleazy strip club that King owned but did not even put any time in it. I saw the potential of the place and decided to offer King a hundred thousand for the place but he declined and said he needed double. Of course, he did, it wouldn't have been like him if he made it easy for me. So, I went to Surge and asked for a loan.

"Of course, I can loan you the money, or we could be business partners." He said with a gentle crooked smile. So for months we literally tore the place down and built it up from the ground up. It's probably the most popular place in Baltimore for supernatural beings. I handpicked most of my girls and I was very particular. I may have created a few enemies in the process due to shallow minds thinking my decisions were all based on looks. None of that mattered to me, I was only interested in having people with good intentions and good energy in my club. Some of the girls that did not get offered a job got very offended and convinced themselves that I thought they were just too beautiful, that the only explanation for them not getting the job was because I was a hater. But in actuality, as we would be sitting in my office I could sense that they weren't good people.

We don't have many rules here but my number one rule is discrete feedings. We lived right alongside the humans so we didn't need the attention, so no unnecessary killing of humans. There were too many willing EHS for us to be careless. Those that don't agree with my new stricter rules either left the clan or became rogue. I personally don't use the enlightened humans due to my bloodlust being very strong. Once I start drinking fresh blood, I have a really hard time stopping. For that reason I always drink out of the pouches.

I don't talk about this often but I somehow can sense the energy of a room emitted from the beings. Like if it's filled with people or others, I somehow get an overall sense of how the majority feel. It definitely can get complicated because people are not black and white. So sometimes I can feel negative energy from a person but It could be because their dog is sick or they are really worried about a family member, but not because they are just in general a miserable sad person. Tricky. But this feeling is how I knew which guards in King's organization I would be able to trust when it came time to overthrow him.

I sat in the deepest corner of the club with Surge trying not to be seen. Leera, a cute Spanish waitress I hired about two years ago came over with my black berry martini. She handed Surge a ginger ale. My eyebrows went up but I didn't say anything.

"Don't worry about me boss you know I never drink on the clock."

"But that's just it Surge, I told you I didn't need you here tonight on duty. We are just here to see how the club is going and make sure that white lily drug doesn't end up in one of my girls." I slid back into the comfy recliner like seating and took a big gulp of my drink. Kitty's time had a total of twenty-nine employees, all of which I felt responsible for. It was a small but efficient club with really good retention. After talking with Red and Allegra I did some digging. White lily was a new drug going around in the supernatural community. Apparently, it started in one of the Central Europe clans which consisted of Greece, Romania, Germany, Poland, France and some surrounding areas near them. There were six main clans as well as some small rogue clans that we knew little about. White lily was sort of like PCP in the human community. The drug made vampires feel extra strong and indestructible. It was very dangerous because we had been living amongst humans centuries and only had one maybe two major incidents where attention was drawn to our kind. This drug was making so many vampires feel superior to humans and as a result, they wanted them to respect us or fear us and bow down. Just the thought of it all was exhausting.

I took a sip of my margarita as a blonde head lady approached me. *How did she know we were here?* Reece used a spell to zip us inside and we told Leera and the bartender not to let anyone know we were here, because once the employees know the bosses are here their actions become less natural and more rehearsed. Also, we were sitting in a specially made area of the club I designed with the architect that allowed us to see the staff but they couldn't see us. So this was weird to say the least. Surge was on his feet before I could even blink.

"I don't mean to intrude." this lady came floating in. I literally never really seen her legs move but she was in front of me now. What the hell is happening?

"I was hoping for a minute to chat with Blue. My name is Alexandria and I have important information. The future of vampires depends on you." She had blonde hair in a short bob, light sky-blue eyes, and soft pink lips. She was very pretty.

"Blue isn't seeing anyone tonight. If you are having issues call the emergency number or wait until Monday. Can't you see…" Surge suddenly froze in the middle of his sentence and passed out. I stood up and looked from him to her. My eyes narrowed.

"What did you just do?" I asked through a tight jaw. Whoever this witch was, I was ready to break her neck with my bare hands and not think twice about it. Surge was my family, everyone knew that. Which meant whatever she needed to talk about better be very important. The energy in this small nook went from laid back to cold and furious but all that was coming from me. I did not feel anything from this witch. That puzzled me since every living thing gives off energy.

TRISTAN CHAPTER 8

I was in bed staring up at my ceiling until the sun went down. I just couldn't sleep these days. The information Tabitha told me has been on my mind. I was actually glad to hear my alarm letting me know it was time to get dressed and become Camilla's brain, and personal shield. At least my mind wouldn't be going into overthinking mode. If only I could speak with my so-called father, but my sister made it seem like he's a dangerous person so maybe it's best I act like I was still ignorant to the situation. I do love my life here but it always felt like something was missing like who was I before I arrived? Did I have a life? I did not know whether I could trust Tabitha or not but she did bring me proof that most of my life was a lie. And if everything she said was true then a lot of my life is a lie. I shuddered at the thought and hopped out of bed and into the shower.

"Camilla's not happy with." Stated Todd, the guard that's always on guard overnight in front of my loft.

"Good morning to you too Todd," I told him. Walking briskly to my bike in the parking garage across from my place.

I sighed deeply when I noticed him catching up to me and continued talking.

"Camilla was informed that you had a guest that no one approved of. She thinks it could be a spy or worse a non-vampire." He said looking for answers in my face so he could undoubtedly be the hero for Camilla.

"I don't know what you are talking about." I finally made it to my bike and peeled off. I do not owe him an explanation. But at least now I know he was on point last night.

I keep wondering why Camilla doesn't see that allowing a few other species into our clan would not hurt us. Her mind is not as political as her dad's was. It would really help strengthen us actually. That's just one of the major differences between Blue's clan and ours. Although we outnumbered their vampires two to one, Blue had something Camilla could never have. What Blue had was loyalty from her people. Whereas Camilla tried to scare people into liking or at least becoming obedient to her. Blue knew how many witches, warlocks, and EHS were in her clan. All of which loved her and not because of fear. They actually adored her for killing King and admired her brilliance. They also noticed the peace her presence brought everyone. Camila will never understand the concept of being a great leader. I hope for my sake it's not her downfall because, like I told her, I will defend her until the end and I intend to keep my word.

I arrived at Camilla's suite earlier than usual so I was not surprised to find her half-dressed. She had on jeans that hugged her so tightly it was a wonder she could walk comfortably. It seems she got stopped midway when getting dressed. Her push-up bra wasn't yet covered by her usual silk blouse and she didn't have on shoes yet. I've seen Camilla like this many times. Her pastel face scrunched up in a serious scowl staring at her phone. Whoever she was on the phone with was seriously working her nerves. I let her acknowledge my presence with a nod and went back into the living room and relieved Gary of the overnight security shift. A pale trustworthy guy. Almost all vampire clan leaders kept a certain amount of security around them at all times. Camila was an extra bundle of nerves due to her father's murder just years before. She had two more regular guards in the hall and a regular dressed one, casually patrolling the area around the suite. My ass barely touched the expensive leather couch cushion when Camilla walked into the living room. Her stilettos making tiny holes in the extra plush carpet. I stood up. Camilla's dark green eyes look me up and down. Camilla was pretty but only from the perfect angle, and in good light.

"Must you always dress like a drug dealer? I pay you more than enough, you should at least be able to wear a pair of slacks and a decent button up shirt." Yea she was definitely annoyed if she started her conversation off with me on that note. I looked down at myself and tried my best not to smile or worse, laugh at the woman that was in charge of hundreds of vampires but couldn't get her own bodyguard to dress properly.

"A white tee and Levi's are never out of style, perfect for any occasion. Besides, I don't know how you would expect me to whoop ass in a tight ass pant suite," I disputed. She put her hand on her non-existent hips and frowned.

"John Wick does it."

"This isn't an action movie Camilla I really have to keep you safe, there are no take two's here." She was still frowned up. She would get a lot further in life if she could at least try to hide her expressions. But she turns red at the drop of hat and I'm not sure if that something she could control. She gets so emotional about the smallest things unlike Blue. Dammit, I was comparing them again.

"I'm sick of arguing with you about this Tristan. And is there something you want to tell me about?" She glared at me.

"Okay, well stop arguing, first off and no there isn't a thing I need to talk to you about. My off time is my off time and none of your rules were broken. But tell me what's up with you." She sighed. I was known for being a bit bossy. Women seemed to love it. Even my boss, though she would never admit it.

"Fine. Some hunters recently discovered the cold bloods clan. You know the stone aged clan in Alaska."

"Yea I've heard about them. They don't use any modern technology really, except a few burner phones. Well, that sucks for them but why are you so upset?" I questioned. She sucked her teeth.

"For one thing the stone aged vampires were some of the oldest, most powerful vampires in the world and they were slaughtered by the dozens which means these hunters are scary maniacs. And two" she held up two manicured fingers, "the cold bloods were responsible for keeping just about all vampire history books. We aren't sure if the hunters found them or not. She walked over to her fridge and grabbed a blood pouch out, inserted a straw and drank as if it were a capri sun.

"Okay so what's in the books Camilla, because nothing you said so far sounds too horrible?" She put her pouch down on the marble kitchen island. She turned pale, well more pale than normal.

"In the books are all of the clan's locations. All our businesses to date, the secrets to how we stay hidden. Stay safe. Basically, they will know how to really annihilate us." My mouth suddenly became very dry and my stomach felt sour. She went on.

"We could get slaughtered in our own beds at any time, or worse they could simply wait until daylight and have our sun blocking systems disabled. We'll be easy targets, being so weakened and frazzled." Even though the sun couldn't really kill us, it could burn turned vampires really bad. It was a horrific thought. I'm not certain anymore about myself, but Camilla and almost everyone in my clan were natural born, but I knew for sure that Blue was a turned vampire. I shuddered at the thought.

"All the major clans have been in communication. We're having one of the biggest meetings in our history in just a few nights." She informed me. My job just got 100x harder. Vampires I could handle. A few angry witches, cool. But a whole race of humans with their advanced technology. Sheesh. How the hell was I supposed to keep us alive? I kept this all to myself. Suddenly the only thing I was concerned about was Blue.

BLUE CHAPTER 9

It took everything in me to unclench my fist, take in a deep breath and not punch this lady so hard it would send her flying and put a hole in my club wall. I finally sat down and collected myself.

"What the hell did you do to him?" I inquired.

"Don't worry, he's fine I just used a simple sleeping spell. Give him twenty minutes, he will be as good as new. Now look, I do not have much time. The great prophecy is finally coming of age and you are in the center of it all."

"Wait, who are you?" I held up an open palm.

"Alexandria, I'm the oldest living witch." She told me. My eyebrows went up because she did not look a day over twenty eight years old.

"I hope you are not serious about all this. I am just *me*, and who really believes in prophecies? They're just man-made tales used to scare us" I told her.

"I can assure you, what I have seen is definitely not man made," She told me.

"How is that, where you there?" I was being a little snarky.

Alexandria was quiet for a minute, just staring right into my eyes as I stared right back. After what felt like forever, she asked me what I felt. A look of surprise came across my face for about a second. Only three people knew about my weird ability to sense the atmosphere and people around me. Many vamps had special abilities, like speed and human mind control. What I could do however, I had never heard of before and that made me cautious about disclosing it.

"I don't know what you are talking about," I told her, not really exuding the same confidence I had just moments before.

"Stop the charade," the blonde head spat. "You know exactly what I am talking about and like I said before, I do not have much time. You have a gift Blue, one that's going to help us all. I have unfortunately seen what is to come in my dreams, or you could call them nightmares."

I do not know why but something in my gut told me I could trust this stranger. The problem with it all was that I still did not feel any energy from this lady in front of me.

"Try again," She said. I looked at her with narrow eyes.

"Are you reading my mind?" I asked her.

"No, but if I were you, I think I would have already tried to feel my energy upon arrival. I had my guard up though so try again." I closed my eyes and sent my energy over to her to feel hers, to feel the room. In her, I felt a sense of urgency and behind that, the truth. All around me buzzed that I was in no danger. The air around me trusted her so I guess I should too. Besides I knew without a doubt in my mind that if she tried something I would end her. Witches need their hands and tongues to do spells and if she crossed me, she wouldn't have either.

"Okay," I finally said, "what do you want from me?" She looked around as if trying to make sure we were alone and couldn't be overheard.

"We are alone besides the sleeping one," I said pointing down at Surge who seemed to be really enjoying the nap. The lights were very low in my club except for the two main stages, but vamps could see everything in here even in low lighting. Which is why I designed the V.I.P. Section a good 20 feet above everything else, like a balcony. I also placed the tables so far back that you could only be seen if you wanted to. Clearly Alexandria did not want to be.

"The prophecy talks about a leader who puts their own fears aside for the good of the clan. A person who has a very good conscience and can actually feel when a person is lying or not. A person who is not afraid or judgmental of others different from herself but instead offers all a safe place to stay. Blue, many witches, warlocks, vampires, and even enlightened humans have been waiting for you."

"Wait. But I cannot tell if a person is lying, I simply feel energy. This so-called gift is being exaggerated trust me." I told her, feeling overwhelmed with it all.

"You don't find it weird that most vampires who are turned, their eyes change maybe one shade lighter. They go from dark brown to maybe hazel, but you Ms. Royal, your eyes went from dark brown to a brilliant blue. Most call that a good omen."

"My name isn't Royal, it's Robinson." Confused as to why the hell she called me that.

"Sorry, I'm ahead of myself here." She pointed a rolled-up piece of old raggedy looking paper on the table in front of us. Read the scroll." But I don't remember ever seeing her with paper in her hand or seeing her place it down on the table. Weird. When I looked up again, she was gone. A few minutes later Surge woke up.

"What did I miss?" He asked while rubbing the back of his neck.

"A lot. She called me Royal which was very strange." He looked away when I said that. "Oh, and apparently I'm supposed to save the world or something of the sort." His eyes widened.

"Well do you believe any of it?" He asked. Until this point, I always thought of Surge as very practical so for him to even ask me that made me a little uneasy.

"I'm not sure," I answered honestly. We read the scroll together.

> When times are bad turn to the cerulean sea
> Think old days aquamarine
> What's hidden will be revealed
> Five is opportune
> Chase the hottest of fires
> Remember strength brings fear
> Fear brings the fight
> Hold hands during the last hour

TRISTAN CHAPTER 10

Nathifa- name means pure

Ekon- name means protector

Kauket- name means goddess of destruction

Kek- name means god of darkness

O dabo olufe mi- means goodbye my love

I woke up gasping for air. But it was so hot and muggy I felt no relief. I really don't remember California air being this hot before, but as I looked around my room nothing looked familiar. It almost looked as if I were in some sort of hut or tent. My brand new wooden floors had been replaced with sand. Where was my desk and MacBook? An old looking book in the corner where my desk should be caught my eye. It had a strange symbol on it. I suddenly realized I wasn't alone, there was a female in the bed next to me. I shook her a little.

"Hey, would you care to wake up and explain what the hell is going on here?" I asked the stranger. Only it wasn't a stranger.

"Blue?" I asked squinting at her. Only it wasn't really Blue. This female looked like her but her eyes were gray and much softer than the Blue I know. Her chin was a little more rounded.

"What the fuck?" Was all I could stamper out at first. After taking a breath I asked.

"Blue, is that you?"

"Ekon, are you okay? Who is Blue?" She asked. She was so beautiful; just as beautiful as the Blue I knew. I looked down at myself. What the hell was I wearing? I didn't have on a shirt and I was wearing was appeared to be a gold and black skirt. This is nuts. I must be going insane.

"No, I'm not okay I-" but I had no time to explain because someone barged in.

"My king, my queen." He bowed quickly. "They have found us! The guards are holding them off but it isn't going well," The guy said. Blue, well the blue look alike jumped up.

"Do not worry Bomani, Ekon and I will take care of this once and for all," She said confidently and calmly. They nodded at each other in understanding.

"Wait what are you all talking about?" I was so confused.

"Come on Ekon, we have talked about this. She threw a handmade spear at me which I caught instinctively as if I had been practicing my whole life for this moment.

"We agreed that next time the bitch came for us we would stand and fight. We are the most powerful beings in the world as long as we are together!" Wow, I could get use to this version of Blue. She was still the confident, strong fighter I was used to but this one apparently loved me back. We stepped outside of the tent thing and something was starting to block out the sun. I quickly realized they were arrows.

"Oh what child's play." Blue's look alike said with a grin. She held up one hand and all the arrows stopped. She twisted her wrist and all the arrows turned around and began flying in the direction they came. Within seconds we heard screams and bodies dropping. Moments later there was a purple mist and very pretty face appeared.

"Oh Nathifa, this is so cute. You really think you have a chance," She said. Oh, so Blue's name is Nathifa in this dream…kinda weird but okay.

"Kauket, we have done this dance so many times before. But this time will be different because I cannot allow you to torture my people anymore. Ekon and I are more powerful than you can even comprehend," Nathifa told her.

"Oh, please spare me!" Kauket flicked her wrist once and sent me crashing into a nearby tent. That's when something in my brain switched and suddenly, I remembered who I was. I was Ekon, Pharoah of Egypt and a powerful sorcerer. I popped up and created an energy ball between my hands. I mentally told Nathifa to move away from Kauket now and a second later she was standing by my side. Wow, we were linked telepathically. I threw my energy ball at our enemy. She held up her hands in an attempt to block it. Nathifa created her own energy ball and threw it at the sorceress. She could not hold that amount of power back. We watched as it almost reached her and put an end to all this. But that's when a black mist appeared and stood in front of Kauket, saving her.

"Kek, my love!" Kauket cried out. Nathifa and I looked at one another.

"Now things are about to get interesting. Ekon hold my hand. We are always stronger together!" Nathifa told me. I eagerly took it. It didn't last long though because Kek threw an energy ball at me much more powerful than Kauket's. That's when everything started to happen in a blur.

"I am the god of Darkness," Kek yelled as the clouds retreated and the sky turned a dark shade of blue, almost black.

"Only fools like yourselves stand up to me and the goddess of destruction! Your time ends today."

"That may very well be true but we will fight to the death before we surrender to you," Nathifa yelled out.

"Very well," Kek smirked.

I picked myself up off the ground just in time to see Kauket and Kek throwing enough energy at Nathifa to kill 500 men. I ran towards her. Apparently, I was fast in this dream. I made it in time to protect her but the feeling of that much power surging into your body, killing you slowly and taking your breath away was bad. But looking into Nathifa's eyes as I fell helplessly was a thousand times worst.

"Habibti, my sweet Blue," I croaked out.

"Shhhhh. Just hold my hand." Nathifa pressed a finger to my lips and grabbed my hand. I noticed we were wearing identical necklaces with blue stones. A single tear fell from her eye. She cried out a tortured scream and began to slump.

"I've loved you since the day we first met. Now I wish I didn't waste so much time being hard to get," I tried to chuckle but it was stifled. "You are stronger than me. You will know what to do!" She whispered while gently stroking my cheek. Something in her eyes told me she was about to do something foolish.

"No," I said. "Don't do this." But it was too late, I could literally feel her essence going into mine. I squeezed her hand. I shouted a spell that I have no idea how I knew. It must have been powerful because Kauket grabbed Kek and they were frozen in time in that embracing position. Statues that would be broken and burned immediately. We did it.

"O dabo olufe mi, we will meet again" I told her as I held her lifeless body.

BLUE CHAPTER II

~~~

Getting dressed was always kinda fun for me. Ever since I could remember, I always kept my closet color coordinated. Even my underwear was folded and organized based on color and style. It just added order and simplicity to my life. I just loved looking nice and neat and today was hair day. I was always keeping my braids touched up.

Sitting in the salon located on the first floor of the Roses, only Reece and I were here today. Reece had been talking for the last ten minutes but I was barely paying attention. I kept finding myself down memory lane more and more lately. Tristan and I had that one great date and a few rendezvous for about a year or so, after that nothing serious; at least that is what I told myself. So for me to keep pondering on the past was really pissing me off. I had so many more important things I should be worried about.

"Ouch. Girl ease up. I thought you would come back from a honeymoon relaxed." I literally only wore my hair one way since I'd been turned. I kept my hair in long braids, that hung all way down to my butt. It's the style I technically died in, so in some weird way, it's the only part of me that reminds me of my old humanity.

"Blue I'm barely touching you. You are still so tender headed. I'm probably the only one who knows you have a weakness... your damn scalp." We both snickered. The two of us always engaged in playful banter. She was such a free spirit, I admired that. I was told I can be a little uptight so we balanced each other out very well.

"Somethings up Blue, you haven't checked neither of your phones in about 15 minutes when usually both your phones are glued to your hands." I was silent; still deep in my thoughts. Her hands were braiding really fast. Once she was done with the plat, she placed the fake hair on an empty salon chair and sat down. She faced me so she could read my face.

Even though I had one of the best unreadable faces one could ask for, Reece and I had been friends since I first arrived at the Roses. She could read my most subtle expression that most people wouldn't even catch. I knew Surge was my guard this shift and was probably right outside the door which was hearing distance to an old vamp like himself. Her dark brown eyes deadlocked on my blue ones. I stared back defiantly because Tristan should not be the topic of discussion on a day like today. I swiveled in the salon chair and stared at myself in the mirror to avoid looking at my best friend.

Contrary to popular belief vamps can see ourselves in the mirror it just wasn't a still image. Our reflection was always wavering. Old witches say it's our souls trying to break free of our bodies because they don't belong in this world anymore. When Reece flicked her wrist, all her bangles clashed and suddenly I was facing her again.

"Reece really?" She never used her powers on me much except that one time we got into a fight with some rogue vamps, but that was to protect me. So this shocked the hell out of me. She stared. Then again, this was Reece we were talking about and she could be a little erratic.

"Reece, I have to attend a meeting with the most important vampires of the world." Accompanying me will be Surge of course, and ten other guards considering that the vampire universal law stated that if you kill a clan leader you could take over and rule their clan. That is why I had to kill King. For this reason, many clan leaders avoid meetings and such, it's very nerve-wracking and honestly kinda scary.

"I need to be very focused on this, we will be heading to the airport tonight." But I was lying. My mind was lost in thoughts of a black ginger with a caramel complexion, focused and driven man who was amazing in bed (even though I've never told him). Behind all his antics and beautiful dimple filled smile he was a calm man who was a natural protector. Ugh!

"Surge, can you run and grab some extra packs of O blood for the trip?" We already had plenty already packed, but I didn't need Surge to hear that I was clearly cracking under pressure.

"Yea, I got you. Be back in five." I waited until I heard the elevator coming down to take him up.

"Okay fine. I can't seem to get my shit together. Tristan..." I said his name through gritted teeth, "has been in my thoughts way too much."

"Seriously Blue. Is it really that bad that you have been thinking about Tristan? I mean you run a club, a clan, and you don't even have a treasurer or even an accountant, which is nuts. You are overworked, all work and no fun. You never even gave him a chance."

"Okay for one, I have no time for a boyfriend." I used my fingers to count off and really drill my point in.

"Two, I am doing an amazing job keeping all numbers all by myself. I can trust myself. Three, Tristan is second in command to a clan leader that hates my guts for absolutely no reason. Doesn't get much messier than that."

"Well, that bitch is a hater point blank PERIOD." She was so extra with that last word but I let her continue. "But seriously that's not the kinda love you can run from. You two are destined to be together whether you believe it or not. He is to you what Micah is to me, he's your Anam Cara as we like to say in the witch community."

"My what?"

"He is your soulmate," She said gently.

"Okay, enough about Tristan. You have been on your honeymoon so I haven't had time to talk to you about Alexandria. A witch I met at my club the other night. It was so weird, she just appeared out of nowhere and had the clearest crystal-like blue eyes, and she had blonde hair." Reece had finished my braids. I was laying my edges down with an edge brush in the mirror. I turned around and Reece looked like she had seen a ghost. She stood frozen for like another three seconds until finally, I couldn't take it anymore.

"Reece what is wrong with you?" Reece had a very fair complexion with a pretty round face, round cheeks, and full lips. She always wore nude lipstick that really complimented her skin tone. She was very curvy, a little thicker than I was.

"You don't mean THE Alexandria. The oldest most powerful that ever lived?" I was surprised by her question.

"Yea she did tell me she was the oldest witch but I did not really believe her. She did not even look thirty." Reece sat down heavily in a salon chair. A group of young girls walked in, spoke to us, and began setting up. The salon was available for use by anyone who lived here.

"Let's go to my apartment. I need a drink." I followed Reece to the elevators. She lived a few floors below me. Once in her apartment, I sat down in her living room on her chesterfield sofa that I picked out for her. Her apartment was much more comfortable and cozier than mine, with warm colors and a very lived in feel to it. She grabbed some summertime watermelon ciroc off the counter and poured two shots. She looked at me like she was about to start talking then got up to pour herself another shot.

"Okay Reece you probably should slow down," I told her. Witches are human at the end of the day, so she was about to be drunk before noon. Though it wouldn't be the first time.

TRISTAN CHAPTER 12

I woke up in a cold sweat, I was breathing heavily. I really had the urge to cry out but I did not. *That was just a really bad dream* I told myself. I would never allow Blue or Nathifa or whoever to sacrifice herself. And what was the language I was speaking in? Arabic? I had so many questions. I decided to get dressed and search for answers. My MacBook was still out getting repairs. Here in the mountains, we had a huge expansive library. I could start my research by looking to see if there was someone named Ekon and Nathifa even though I knew it was a stretch. I was hoping I perhaps learned about them from a history channel or something.

Once I arrived at the library, I was relieved to find it almost empty. I really didn't want to have to explain that I had a horrible nightmare and was attempting to do research on some people I only just heard of in a dream. I was in the library for a good three hours and to my surprise, I had stumbled upon lots of information regarding the two. They were royalty and protectors of people hundreds of years ago. I clicked on the page that had a very old drawing of the two and the image was haunting. There we were, just as we looked in my dream. We even had the matching necklaces on that I noticed. I wanted to continue my research, but in my peripheral vision I noticed Camilla's cousin walk into the library. Her office was located in here. If she spots me, I knew I would be asked a million and one questions by Camilla. I decided I should just leave now. I left out in a hurry after I wiped the memory on the computer clean.

I met Andre and Terrell at a small bar in the caves. I was planning on talking to them about my so-called sister Tabitha.

"Hey bro? You look terrible!" Andre told me. Terrell elbowed him to shut up.

"What?" He needs to get over Blue already he's really tripping," Andre said. He's been this blunt since I first met him years ago.

"If you would just shut the hell up, I could tell you why I asked y'all to meet me here," I told them feeling annoyed.

"I may be a natural born," I told them. It took some convincing, which I can understand. But after showing them I could read the ancient language they finally believed me.

"That's not even the best part," I took the picture Tabitha gave me out of my pocket and showed them.

"Bro, this is wild news. I'ma need a drink!" Terrell exclaimed. After throwing back several shots, I left the bar and went home to crash. I was just getting settled in my favorite chair when I found a letter under my door.

I couldn't get this message to Blue, so you were my next best option. I need help. The humans have me captured. They are called the green group. They are driven by fear and are very wicked to the core. All they care about is remaining on top of the food chain. This group is a threat to anyone that isn't human. It's only a matter of time before they realize I got this message out. Please be vigilant. Please help blue.

Sincerely, the White Witch.

I wanted to reread it, but as soon as I got to the bottom of the letter it disappeared in a cloud of smoke.

"What the hell?" I said out loud. Suddenly there was a knock on my door. Damn, *what could it be now?* I was very surprised to see Lolli, the newest member of the Cali clan at my door. I did not trust this guy but I was very curious about why he was here. I opened the door and waited for him to speak. He looked like he just walked out of the movie Grease.

"I know you're probably wondering why I'm here," he said as he slicks his hair back nervously.

"Yea and you have five seconds to start explaining." I told him with my hand on my glock. He put his hands up. His small frame was non threatening but I never underestimate people.

"Let me start by saying I was your moms best friend. I made her a promise when you were first born that I'd do everything I can to protect you."

"Does it look like I need protection?" I asked him. He continued without answering my question.

"We had to keep you hidden and we were doing great for the first eight years of your life. Then the next thing I knew you were sent away, your mom did not tell me the details but I'm guessing the evil Helda, who is the Kings wife was starting to have suspicions. Not to soon after you were gone your mom was killed. I really wasn't in a great mental space and I was so comfortable where I was. I was selfish and I didn't hold onto my promise I made to her. I now realize that I have to uphold my promise. And doesn't the saying goes better late than never? Are you going to gonna invite me in?" He asked me. I'm still trying to figure this all out whether he's telling the truth or not but I stand to the side and allow him to come in.

"I'm supposed to just believe that you knew my mom?" I asked him.

"No, that's why I'm going to show you. Open up your mind," he tells me as he places two fingers on his temple. Before I knew it images were flashing in my mind of a beautiful young lady with wild hair running through a courtyard, the only black person in sight. A very young looking Lolli chasing behind her. I hear sentence fragments… best friends, I love you like a brother, trust. I witnessed the two grow up in the castle together but as they grew older Lolli's feelings were no longer just platonic. He let go of his temple.

"You get the point now?" He asked smiling uncomfortably.

"First of all cool powers." I told him.

"Now let me get this straight, so you fell in love with my mom but she was in love with my dad, who is the king and you were always afraid to say anything. So then you felt some resentment that I wasn't your son and that's why you're just now showing up in my life. Wow! I could've really used you all these years not knowing anything of my history or of my mom. And all this time you were supposed to be here for me." I was a little surprised by my reaction. I walked over to my fridge and grabbed a beer, I just needed a minute to gather my thoughts.

"What can I say I'm selfish, and I don't see the point in putting myself on the line for others. But even though I'm the total opposite of you, with your mom gone you are the only family I have."

BLUE CHAPTER 13

~~~

Why was Reese so spooked? After throwing her last shot back we both were seated on the couch.

"Okay whatever Alexandra told you take heed. She doesn't visit anyone often but when she does it's always to deliver a powerful message that must not be taken lightly."

"Well, she mentioned something about..." I began

"No don't say anything! Because I'm a witch you can't tell me. I'm so sorry Blue. I wish I could listen and help you, but this journey is all your own," Reece told me. "Alexandra is like the mother of all witches. We call her the white witch. No one knows exactly how old she is, but thousands of years old for sure. And most of us witches die wishing to meet her. I would love to meet her but not anytime soon." I suddenly got distracted. I felt heat and a slight breeze on my shoulder.

"What the hell, Reece do you feel that?" I looked behind me. It was the white witch. I spun around. This time the witch had on a long flowing white gown. It was beautiful, I wondered if it was a Vera Wang gown.

"I don't have much time, it takes a lot of power for me to send my form here from where I am."

"Where are you?" I asked.

"There is no time for that," She said. I looked over at Reece, she was fast asleep.

"What the hell another sleeping spell?" Something was very weird. The vibe in the room was off or should I say missing. Then I noticed she was floating in the air.

"My child is fine. I would never harm her but she cannot see me yet. For another witch to see me, it usually means their death. I don't have much time. You must be very careful tonight Blue. Enemies will be near you. Use your ability. Only you will be able to bring back balance and save us all. When something feels right Blue, it's right." She turned around to look behind her. "They're coming now I must go."

I didn't see anything behind her. What the hell just happened? This lady just came in and gave me a whole riddle to solve. She was the mother of burdens. I suddenly felt ill. This was a lot for someone who loves to be in control to take in. I'm dealing with a witch full of riddles that can astral project, my best friend can't help me, and I couldn't seem to find my focus. Her warning made me think. I was getting on a private plane in a few hours so that I would be in the caves in time for the meeting tomorrow night and the only people who were going to be around me were *MY* people. So, who is it around me that can't be trusted?

TRISTAN CHAPTER 14

Between the letter being on my mind, my so-called sister visiting me and informing me that I am supposed to be a Royal, I just couldn't get any sleep. There was only one voice I wanted to hear. Even though it's been a little while I just knew she would pick up. The phone rings three times before she does.

Blue- "Hello"

Tristan- "Hey Blue, it's Tristan."

Blue- "What do you want?" *I have a strange feeling that she's not happy to hear my voice.*

Blue- "We agreed not to talk anymore."

Tristan- *Ouch, I'ma play it cool though.* "Well actually YOU agreed we wouldn't talk and YOU cut ME off. Even though the last time we were together, it was fantastic." *I still don't get why she's so damn standoffish.*

Blue- "Was it really though? What did we really expect would be our outcome with you being second in command to a narcissist idiot across the country?"

Tristan- "I thought love conquers all... Anyway, I didn't call you to argue."

Blue- "Okay well what do you want?

Tristian- *I want you.* "Have you heard about what happened to the cold one's clan?"

Blue- "Of course. I will be leaving tomorrow."

Tristan- "Oh okay I was just making sure you were in the loop."

There was an awkward silence for about five seconds.

Tristan- "Okay well nice chat." *Not really but whatever.*

Blue- "Yea well thanks for the concern."

Tristan- "Bye, well wait there is something else." I was still having a tug a war in my brain as to whether to fill her in on everything I just found out or not.

Blue- "Okay what is it?"

Tristan- "You know what, it's nothing. Just be safe." *She has enough on her plate.*

Blue- "Yea, okay. Goodbye."

The phone conversation with Blue took an awkward turn which I should have expected. I wanted to tell her about the dream but I couldn't. I wanted to tell her about the letter, but not over the phone. Most of all I wanted to know how she would feel about this Lolli character showing up.

Blue was unlike any other female I met. She always kept it real with me and was so self assured. When you find a woman that's not only is sexy as hell, but can also hold great conversations with then she's a keeper. That is why I feel like she should be mine. But instead, she wanted to cut me completely out of her life and really hasn't looked back in two years. Meanwhile, I still can't connect with any other female the way I did with her.

I felt like I was the female in the situation, *oh hell no*! I had to man up. I ran out to the kitchen and cracked an egg and was about to eat it raw to succumb to my male ego but I knew that was being irrational. Also, if I did it, I'd be hurling afterwards. I threw the egg away and hit the punching bag in my spare room instead. After my workout I grabbed a pouch of O- blood out of the fridge. I drank the blood in 2.5 seconds and hopped in my marble tile shower. *I am so ready for this night to be over.*

BLUE CHAPTER 15

~~~

Phone rings. *Why the hell is Tristan calling me?* I thought as I reached for my vibrating phone.

Blue- "Hello"

Tristan- "Hey Blue, it's Tristan." *Duh, I have your number still saved.*

Blue- "What do you want? We agreed not to talk anymore." *That came out a bit sharper than I meant it to.*

Tristan- "Well actually *YOU* agreed we wouldn't talk and *YOU* cut *ME* off. Even though the last time we were together was fantastic."

Blue- "Was it really though? What did we really expect would be our outcome with you being second in command to a narcissist idiot across the country?" *I have to keep him at a distance.*

Tristan- "I thought love conquers all... Anyway, I didn't call you to argue."

Blue- "Okay well what do you want?" *Damn, I sound cold.*

Tristian- "Have you heard about what happened to the cold one's clan?"

Blue- "Of course. I will be leaving tomorrow."

Tristan- "Oh okay I was just making sure you were in the loop."

There was an awkward silence for about five seconds.

Tristan- "Okay well nice chat."

Blue- "Yea well thanks for the concern."

Tristan- "Bye, well wait there is something else."

Blue- "Okay what is it?"

Tristan- "You know what, it's nothing just be safe." *He's hiding something I can hear it in his voice.*

Blue- "Yea, okay. Goodbye."

I hung up the phone very annoyed. I need to be making my way downstairs to my ride. Instead, I was staring at my phone feeling stuck. I haven't heard that voice in two years. I broke it off with him because who wants to do a long-distance relationship? Not only that but look at who he works for. That right there was a huge conflict of interest. I'm trying to run an entire clan community opposite of how his clan is ran. I decided to go to my favorite place in the Roses which is the art room on the basement level. I needed to sculpt, get my hands dirty so that I could get my mind off of Tristan. But even after setting up my clay and wheel, my mind found its way back to him and I. The deep red hues of the clay reminded me of his hair.

I first met him at a meeting I had with Mr. Brinks (Camilla's dad) about five years ago and I was totally unimpressed. He was just standing there and looked very out of place like his mind wasn't really with us at all. I got a strong feeling of disinterest from him but I barely gave him a second thought. My thoughts were very much on the issue I was dealing with at the time. I was there to try and ask for safe passage for some witches that were seeking refuge at the Roses, but had to come through the caves and would need shelter for a few nights. I heard Mr. Brinks was a very fair man but Camilla was not.

When I arrived at the meeting, Surge and I sat down at the round table. Across from us sat Mr. Brinks. To his right was Tristan and, on his left, Camilla. We both had additional guards standing behind us, you could never be too safe when dealing with vampires. The meeting that hadn't even started yet but, Tristan took a call and then rushed out. Apparently, this meeting bored Camilla as she sat and filed her nails. Wow how rude and not to mention unprofessional. I didn't even give her a glance. She was acting like a child and I don't have much patience for children. Lucky for me, Mr. Brinks was alive and in charge at this time so the meeting went well and I returned home. I wondered how can one have a child that comes out nothing like you. Maybe she took more after her mother.

A few weeks after the meeting, I was home getting ready to start my day when I received a knock on the door from one of my guards. He said I had a visitor. I did not like surprises and I've made it well known. We are the only clan that kept pets. That is just one reason why I hate surprise visitors because other vampires tend to kill animals for either blood or sport. Just the thought of someone coming near my home and harming my Moo moo was enough to get my blood boiling hot. I'd have their head on a spike before they even knew I was on their trail. I shook the thought out of my head because no one could be that dumb right?

"Well, who exactly is it and what do they want?" I asked my guard. I knew it wasn't a human because they would have never made it up past the receptionist on the 1st floor.

"Not sure boss. Some light skin vampire that says he only wants to talk to you. I think we should send him home though. He can't just come to the Roses unannounced. Let alone come to your suite."

"You're right Eli," Micah said as he walked in. "But I want to let him in and I want him to try something with Blue, so I can beat the shit outta yo."

"Micah, we don't treat our guest that way and we shouldn't assume this guy wants trouble," I told him firmly but they could tell I was annoyed as well. Send him in. Only an idiot would try something with all of us standing here.

"Erin," I looked at my guard who I had just hired a few months ago. He was a tall brown haired Italian warlock. He was nothing special on the eyes. "Make sure all of our pets are put up."

"Yes boss," He left out with a nod. I never got a bad feeling from Erin but for some reason the other guards gave him a hard time and I'm not sure why. The Roses was like a melting pot and I loved the changes I made around in just the few years since I've been clan leader. The Vamp walking in snapped me back into attention.

"You don't have to put the pets up for me. I don't bite," He grinned a flashy fanged filled smile. Ugh he was very annoying, cocky, and worst of all very good looking. I have only been with one vampire ever and he got murdered by a rogue vampire in a fight while we were out in Queens, New York at a party. The fact that I couldn't get to him fast enough to save him still haunts me to this day. Ever since then, I decided my businesses and my clan would take up all my focus and energy. I swore off dating. I couldn't protect him but I will protect my clan. Men were the last thing I should be worried about. So why is this man here? I eyeballed my guest.

"You are Mr. Brinks second in command, why are you here without sending notice first?" I stood directly in front of him, staring him in the eyes.

"Well, actually I work for Camilla now. Mr. Brinks was killed last week, unfortunately." He looked genuinely sad for a moment.

We all stood around my living room. Two guards stood behind me near the kitchen area, two were to my left near my tv and Micah was two feet from my side ready to leap. It was very impressive I knew, but I never took advantage of my power. I gave Micah the 'don't do anything look.' Not that it always worked with him since he was a live wire. A gang member in his former human life. He was loyal to a fault, and willing to die for the people he loved if it ever came to that. I looked at Micah then my surprise visitor and I noticed they were similarly dressed. They both were super casual in blue jeans, white tee shirts, and foamposites.

"I'm sorry what is your name again?" I asked him.

"Oh wow, you don't even remember my name? I'm so hurt." He was smiling and holding his chest. He walked over to the minibar by the fireplace and poured himself a shot of rum. Oh wow, yea he was a cocky one.

"I literally met you for ten seconds," I said, while rolling my eyes.

"I'm Tristan and yes I am Camilla's second in command. I am here unannounced because I wanted to surprise you." He threw his shot back.

"Everyone who knows Blue, knows she hates surprises," Micah said with his bottom lip turned up slightly in disgust. His arms were folded in front of him. If we were outside, I'm hundred percent sure Micah would have spat on the ground near Tristan's feet. If Tristan noticed the disdain, he didn't let on.

"Well, I'm here to try and get to know her." He was looking at me as if I were the most delicious piece of chocolate cake; the last piece and he hadn't eaten in days. My brown skin attempted to blush but I shook it off. I kept my cool because he wasn't about to come in here and woo me. But his intense gaze took me by surprise. I haven't had a man make me feel like this since I was human. I let my senses check him out and I felt no threat from him. I cleared my throat and I sent all the guards away. Of course, Micah wasn't happy but he would never show disrespect in front of an outsider. He just gave me a look and then looked at Tristan in the eye. They were about the same height.

"I won't be far at all," He said and left out.

"I'm sure she can handle herself," Tristan shot back.

"Oh, you have no idea," I said as I turned to face him.

"I'm sorry you came all this way but I am not interested in dating at the moment. I'm involved in too many things to even be thinking about dating," I told him. I liked to get straight to the point and I didn't feel like having company any longer.

"Wow just like that? So you're all business and no play, or do you just think I'm ugly?" He grinned a dimple filled smile. Oh he wasn't ugly, this man was uniquely gorgeous. He had perfect caramel skin with a few freckles. He had beautiful hazel eyes and his copper red hair was in a sharp low cut. I almost asked for his skincare regime. He was the perfect height to about 6'2".

"It has nothing to do with your looks I said wiping down my counters to keep my hands busy. I literally have no free time and besides you live halfway across the country. I'm sorry I'm just not interested," I said.

"Well okay, imma get outta your way. I see you're busy and I don't want you to send your little goons in after me," He said but I knew he wasn't worried about any of them, even though he should be. He left after pouring yet another shot but that was far from the last time I'd hear from Tristan. For two weeks straight he sent gifts to my house. Very good taste in perfume and jewelry. But I was very well off and not easily impressed. It was on the fourteenth day that the gift was merely a card. A small red card. On the front it read 'for a beauty'. I opened it and inside was all blank except for the black small print that said 'Get dressed. No heels; jeans and a tee shirt will do.' I threw the card down.

Who does he think he is? But before I knew it, I was dressed casually. And surprisingly enough, I was having one of the best times of my life. He took me out to a gun range, go cart racing and then a museum. I felt a little underdressed in the museum but I fit right in for the most part which was refreshing.

When we pulled up to the Roses he said,

"You looked like you needed to let your hair down and have some fun, I hope tonight you got to do just that." He rubbed his thumb along my chin and jawline. Before I knew it or gave it to much thought. I kissed him sweetly and said,

"Thank you."

He didn't try to walk me to my apartment, instead we simply said our goodbyes in front of my building, and I walked away, allowing my hips to slightly sway more than I normally would.

TRISTAN CHAPTER 16

~~~

L ooking around, I must say, my man cave is the shit. But I couldn't help but wonder what my crib would look like if I lived amongst the Royals.

"Alexa play Kevin Gates," once my music was on, I got cleaned up. I went to my walk-in closet. I had a tennis shoe collection that would rival the celebrities, well honestly, I probably have more.

I can't believe it took me two weeks to book her. Ever since I went all the way across the U.S. those few years ago to surprise Blue, I can't get her out of my mind. Our date was so amazing. I knew she had an amazing time too but at the very end of the night, she text me *I'm sorry I can't do this.* We did end up going steady for a good year and it was a little messed up at times because of the long distance but it was still the only serious relationship I've been in. It's been two years since then. It's like she has a life mission to resist me. She wasn't like that in the dream.

For the first time in my life, a girl had me so wrapped up. Of course I've been sleeping with women and even dating some of them since our breakup. They are only good for sex if that. It's like I just cannot get into them. It would all be so much easier if I didn't believe that she does love me. When it was just her and I together it was like she was all I needed and I know she felt the same. But as soon as we were around other people it's like she remembered she had to be the strong leader. When did a woman having a man become a weakness? I honestly did not understand it and trying to just pissed me off more. Her thug life guards pissed me off too when we first met but I never let them see me sweat.

My focus needs to be less about Blue and more about Camilla's safety. We will have a dozen of the vampire leaders here at the caves tonight so this was not the time to let my guard down. Out of all the clans in the world, the two United States clans were very sought after. The caves being number one, because we were bigger and the mountains were more beautiful than the life in the city, but the life in the city had its perks too. The USE clan was powerful and thanks to Blue it was becoming more and more popular and respected more than ever before. I finished getting dressed and headed to Camilla's crib. She was shirtless again and also pant-less this time. She wasn't alone. Her cousin Ava, who was also the caves treasurer was here as well.

"I have no idea what to wear to this freak show," Camilla complained.

"Seriously you're overthinking it, you need to be your normal business chic self," Ava told her.

"Why is this any different than usual?" Ava had a puzzled look and then she looked at me and then back to Camilla. Camilla gave me a look and blushed.

"Because that thick blue-eyed girl will be there," She spat. Knowing full well Blue's name.

"I'll be in the living room," I said already walking down the hall, tired of looking at her chicken legs. I really would like to have the effect on Blue that I seem to have one every other female that I've met.

"I really don't know what he sees in her, you are way prettier than she is." Her cousin said pumping her head up. It wasn't true of course. Not to me. I could look at Blue's face all day. She had one of the best poker faces I've ever seen but if you stare in her eyes deep enough you will see her true feelings before she has a chance to hide it. After Camilla and Ava decided on an outfit, I had to admit that for a slim chick she looked cute today. Her button up shirt complimented her chestnut hair, which Ava had pinned up for her. We were now on our way out the door heading to the meeting.

"Okay, so I need you to always be at my right side Camilla. I shoot best from this angle."

"Whatever Tristan. Just make sure my hair is perfect if I die." I knew she was joking but I hated when she made shallow jokes like that. That's one reason why I never thought of her more than a boss or a little sister. We made our way down the halls and outside to the black limousine. I kept catching Ava looking at me. I was familiar with that look. If we make it through this meeting without anyone killing us, I know Ava would want to be in my bed in the a.m. Then I'll be making up an excuse as to why she has to leave and why I don't want to go to breakfast or explain that I don't want coffee or even more sex. Right now, I had no time for her flirting. I needed to focus.

I always get into super serious mode when I was protecting Camilla. There was a reason I was second in command. No one in the caves was on my fighting level skills. All natural born vampires have some sort of skill or heightened sense. I always considered myself a turned vampire that was blessed with abilities. But now I wasn't so sure if what Tabitha said had truth to it or not. I was a lot faster than most vampires and I'm talking lightning speed. Sort of like the flash from the justice league I like to think. I have to really focus to move that fast. The flash made it a little too easy. It also drains a lot of my energy but I have a duffel bag packed with first aid, extra blood, energy drinks, burner phones, candles and smoke signals. I had to be prepared for whatever because it was my job. I paid attention to every detail and because of that, I saved Camilla and her dad from a very well-planned assassination back when Mr. Briggs was still clan leader. Too bad I was out of town when the second attempt was successfully made. That's how I got to be where I am today. I just hope for Blue's sake, Surge and Micah we're on point tonight because if anything happened to her...

"Are you okay?" Camilla asked looking puzzled and then annoyed.

"I really hope you didn't do any drugs knowing how serious this is." I was shaking my head trying to get Blue from my thoughts. I hadn't noticed Camilla and Ava watching me like a hawk.

"I'm fine. When the hell have you known me to do drugs Camilla? You just be saying anything," I told her shaking my head.

"Well, whatever is going on you need to focus. I was joking earlier about dying you know?"

"I know. Don't question my ability to protect you. You've never done that before so don't start now."

"Okay." she sighed and looked out her window. As much as she worked my damn nerves, I know it would eat me alive if I ever let anything happen to her.

BLUE CHAPTER 17

The time finally arrived for me to make my way to the caves. I never announced which of my guards will be accompanying me on this trip. I knew Surge and Micah automatically assumed they would both be going with me. I decided one of them should definitely stay home to watch over the Roses along with Reese. She was still in shock over the whole white witch thing. I promised her I would really focus on the whole thing once I returned. There wasn't enough time right now.

I know I'm a strong, and fair leader to my clan, but only an idiot would believe there weren't some vampires, witches, and maybe even humans that wanted me dead. This meeting would be dangerous and I was just ready to get it over with. I summoned twenty guards to my apartment, mainly veterans but I had a few new ones in the mix so that they could gain some experience. I gave them all orders. Eight will be accompanying me and the other men will stay here to watch out for an invasion or anything out of the ordinary. Micah was going with me. Surge was in charge here. He wasn't happy but

I only saw the disapproval on his face for about one second before he got it together.

"All right, so everyone heard her, let's move now!" Surge was much better than me at giving out orders. Micah and Surge were almost equally matched with fighting and gun skills but I picked Micah to accompany me because of his temper. He was more hot headed than Surge. I'd rather have Micah where I could see him. Erin was going to be the driver today. We were heading out to the airport. Once inside the SUV, I poured myself a glass of blood. I wanted to be full at the meeting. A hungry belly was an easy distraction. But after two sips I started to feel a little odd and decided I didn't want any more blood.

"Micah, does this blood taste old or something to you?" I asked him.

"What you say K'ly?" He slurred out.

I frowned. He never called me by my birth name in all the years I've known him. Something wasn't right here. Suddenly I felt fear. My powers were tingling but they felt very dull. I looked up slowly because the vibrations of disloyalty, betrayal, and (unfortunately for me) success, were coming ever so slightly from the driver seat. Erin and I met eyes in the mirror. The cold look in his eyes along with the evil grin told me everything I needed to know. That's when I thought back to hiring day. As soon I walked into the room last year to interview Erin something told me not to trust him. I decided to go against it but I can't recall why. Then the next time I met him everything was great. Which is weird because it really isn't like me to even do a second interview or give second chances. I had pushed my powers back wanting to believe I was just out of whack because I wasn't getting much sleep. Now that I've thought about it, I never felt anything when Erin was standing too close to me.

"This isn't the way to the airport. You disabled my powers somehow. What the fuck did you do to me? Pull over now Erin," I told him.

"Sorry boss I can't do that, see technically I don't work for you. But good for you, finally admitting out loud that you have a gift." He sneered.

"Well, who do you work for?" I asked.

"Oh you remember Alyssa, the pretty redhead that Camilla cast away from her clan because she's a witch. She came to the Roses looking for sanctuary but you did not allow her to join your clan because you were intimidated by her powers. You know, women pretend that they like to uplift one another but they really don't," He explained looking so smug.

"I was never afraid of her power. I just knew she had ill intentions and she's mentally deranged. She uses dark magic. She's not to be trusted and apparently you aren't either."

"Imma kill you for this," slurred Micah. But he was fighting to keep his eyes open. Erin busted out laughing.

"You two should see yourselves." Apparently Micah had drank much more of the poison than I did. So did my guard in the front seat. He was totally knocked out.

"What the hell did you use to drug us?" I was still calm which was surprising but I'm sure it has something to do with this poison.

"Well boss." he kept emphasizing the word boss to be a smart ass. "Alyssa made a batch of a drug called white lily."

"I've heard about it actually."

"Yea but you don't know everything! This drug can be modified. Each batch created can cause a different reaction. We can create angry vampires or sleepy vampires." He was grinning ear to ear.

"So, what's going on with the batch we have taken?" I asked him.

"In small doses, this particular batch makes you tired and dulls your senses and if you have special abilities," he looked at me through the mirror again "it dulls them as well. That's why every time on my shift, if you were in tune with yourself, you would have realized your powers weren't working. But since you're more afraid of your ability than inviting of it you made my job easy." He was still rambling on and on about easy and it was to keep the white lily in my home and how trusting I was. It made me a little sick. Then went on about Surge and Micah being all bark and no bite.

"You know basically Blue, I got a job with you just so I can keep up with your whereabouts and learn how you move. Just like you did with king. Did I mention King was Alyssa's lover?" He asked me.

"So you have worked for me for over two years and all this time you've been conspiring against me?" I asked him realizing I really messed up.

"Yup," He replied. We were going about 100 mph then suddenly there was a huge explosion behind us. The flames were so high and caused a multi car accident. It was the other SUV that was following us. My men. Four dedicated and loyal men! My chest burned with pain and anger.

"You're gonna pay for this with your life!" I told him gritting my teeth is anger. I tried to grab my phone so I could text Surge but of course, I didn't have service. We appeared to be crossing the Bay bridge. *Where was he taking us.*

"You must think we're idiots. Alyssa and I have been planning this for over two years. She hates you. This will end badly for you." His voice was so cheerful, he was so repulsive. I can't wait to take his throat out. I had my head down slightly. I felt disgusted with it all and disappointed in myself. How could I have been tricked so easily? My eyes looked up at him,

I was glaring so hard he looked away. Even with this drug in my body I knew I was still deadly. I've been underestimated as well as made a fool of. We continued riding. He quickly lifted the glass that divides the backseats and the front seats in my luxury SUV. I continued to stare at him through the mirror until the glass was completely up and I was left looking at myself in the dark glass.

TRISTAN CHAPTER 18

Since we lived here at the caves, I expected us to be the first ones here to attend this meeting. I was actually kind of counting on it. But judging by the parking lot of the antiquated multipurpose building I could tell we weren't. Camilla had hired Sue, a cave local who did the catering and decorating for parties. She literally only worked about ten days out of the year but Camilla paid her substantially well. Too much money was wasted on Sue in Ava's opinion, but who else was going to set up a six-foot-high wine glass display in a perfect pyramid shape or make fancy little sandwiches that never got touched but looked nice, or order the best imported aged blood wine. Sue had outdone herself this time. Pulling into the parking lot there were huge fancy balloon arches. Once inside the huge conference hall there was a glass pyramid in the center of the room as well as ice sculptures and a small blood fountain. I don't want to think about where all the blood came from. There was a 'welcome all' sign in English and right below it five other languages. I'm guessing Spanish, French, Hindu, Mandarin and I have no idea the fifth one. The floors have been waxed, everything was sparkly and shiny. Hopefully everything will not soon be covered in blood. Camilla was walking slightly behind me on my right side as I instructed her to. Her high heels clicking on the marble floor. I told her stilettos were not a good choice for today. What if we needed to run?

"Relax," she told me "I'll be fashionable and practical, these are not stilettos. These are chunky heels and I can run in these if I need to." The Cali clan's multipurpose building was located in the center of the caves. There were like five different exits if you knew the layout. To me, it was an easy location for a massacre. The perpetrator, once done with his bidding, would only have an army of about five vampire soldiers to get through the exits if someone decided to kill a clan leader. And Camilla's best men weren't present because we had most of them here with us or protecting her family. We made our way to the largest conference hall about 30 feet from the main door.

Apparently, it was the China/India clan who were the first to arrive. They were a very large clan based out of Xi'an, China. Both the Indian clan leader and Chinese clan leader decided to combine the clans thousands of years ago seeing strength in numbers. Unlike the US clans, most of the other clans don't all live in the same area or even in the same country like we do. Every clan is different though. The China/Indian clan were very powerful and wealthy. Having dealings in two different countries definitely gave them an advantage. The leader of their clan, Zun Lee, was one of the oldest living vampires and was respected by many. There were about half a dozen Chinese men and half a dozen Indians spread out throughout the building. As we reached the hall, I walked in first and I made sure it was safe. Zun Lee stood and we all very politely spoke and took seats around a huge oval table. Well actually Camilla and Zun Lee sat first. I stood behind Camilla along with two of our other men. I had five others spread out throughout the building.

"I'm going to grab a glass of blood wine does anyone want anything?" Ava asked as she slid her fingers down my chest while she walked past.

"I'm fine." I couldn't eat with all this going on.

"I'll take a glass Ava and you can leave your slutty desperation at the door when you return." Camilla snapped.

"Oh sure," Ava said salty as hell. Zun Lee sat very quietly and patiently, his men were like statues. We were all just waiting on everyone else to arrive. I on the other hand felt a little shifty. I was worried about Blue and cursing myself for not bringing more of our men. We didn't have as many as some of the other clans. I texted Blue twice just a simple, You good? As stubborn as she was I never knew her to not respond so I was beginning to feel worse.

I couldn't keep my eyes off my phone. Suddenly I heard another clan approaching. Whoever they were, they were causing quite the commotion. When they entered the conference hall everyone around me bowed their head. Oh shit wait what was going on? Tabitha entered after a dozen guards.

"Please welcome from the Royal clan, Tabitha Royal." One of her men announced. Her crown was beautiful her hands covered in jewels, her hair was up. She looked totally different than the night when she came to visit me. She looked over at me. I began to walk towards her.

"Hey, I—" I was struck in the back of my knees by one of her guards before I could even finish my sentence.

"What the hell?" As I fell, I grabbed the guard's stick and swung at his lower legs making him fall. All her guards were surrounding me, pointing wooden spears at me.

"Let him live. Royals haven't graced the common in decades, he doesn't know the rules of a high society." She sneered and took a seat.

"Of course he doesn't, and your family is to blame for that aren't they?" Lolli appeared out of no where glaring at Tabitha. He slowly made his was around the table and stood beside me.

"I'd watch my tongue Lolli, your mind games may have gotten you out of the castle but they won't work on me. I have no problem killing you where you stand. But then again your life is pathetic so I'd probably be doing you a favor." She chuckled.

"What a bitch, how do you know her?" Camilla whispered to me. That really meant something coming from her. I didn't answer Camilla's question but to answer my own question that I had been asking myself for about a week now as to whether I could trust Tabitha the answer is no, but Lolli may be trustworthy after all.

BLUE CHAPTER 19

We pulled up to some deserted mansion. It was on hundreds of acres of land surrounded by lots of trees. Looks like we were somewhere on the Eastern shore. My hands suddenly pulled together in front of me at the wrists as if they were magnetized. Okay this witch was getting on my nerves now. I did not have to see Alyssa to know she was here. She was trying to show off but making magic handcuffs wasn't even a hard spell. Reese could do that in her sleep. Two large men pulled me out of my SUV.

"Torch it. For all we know her witch friend might be able to track it down somehow with the spell." Erin told one of the large men. Making it the second SUV to be blown up. They were smart, damn. I was brought to my feet then all of the sudden I was seeing stars.

Once I woke up it was dark out. Panic tried to creep in. I took a deep breath and calmed myself. How long have I been missing? Did the meeting proceed without me? I hope not because I really had a lot to say about the problems with the witches; even though this particular witch was bat shit crazy, I knew most of them weren't. I felt some pain in my ankle. A rusted shackle connected to a thick chain on my left leg was cutting into my ankle. I looked down and there was some dried-up blood around the metal. I focused my energy. I closed my eyes and I tried again to relax. This place was so ancient and musty. I did my best to cross my legs. I found that meditation and staying calm always helped me focus and win fights. I opened my eyes and looked around at my surroundings. I hurried up and stood once I realized I was on a filthy cot. Not even jail inmates get treated like this. There was one window, with bars on it, of course. I was in a large dusty room with brown panel walls. There was mice or rat poop all on the cot. I swallow back vomit and inhaled deeply. *Surge is going to find me* I thought to myself as I tried to hush the little voice that also said *Tristan will try to find me too.* I don't know how long that might take or how long I have with these crazy people. I can't depend on that. I need to focus and get out of this as soon as possible. I kicked some dirt and trash from the corner of the room and decided that's where I would sit and try meditating again.

"Blue! Blue is that you? Please tell me you know what the hell is going on?" A familiar voice pleaded.

"Omg Allegra is that you? How the hell did you end up here?"

"Someone grabbed me as I left your penthouse last week. I haven't eaten anything since then." I sent my energy out to see if she was telling the truth. Sadly, she was. Even though I do not care for her I felt horrible that she was here in this mess. I have to get her out of here.

"I'm so sorry."

"Don't be sorry, just be the hero that everyone thinks you are. Oh and don't drink the blood they laced it with some drug." she scoffed.

"White lily," I said more to myself than to her.

"Yea, well whatever it is I only like taking drugs on my own terms." She informed me.

After some time, I heard the keys rattling and someone at my door. I immediately stood. I figured it was Erin or Alyssa, but to my total shock it was Micah. He looked so much better than I felt.

"Micah how did you...?" I began to ask him. He flashed a toothy grin at me exposing the gold grills he had in his mouth. I was never big on affection, and I became even more withdrawn when I became leader, but I gave Micah the biggest hug. He hugged me back for like a second.

"We don't have time for the mushy shit Blue." He was right.

"Erin's dead. I dared him to get closer to me when he came in my room to talk more shit you know, since I'm all bark and no bite. He wasn't as smart as he thought." Just as Micah picked my ankle chain open everything froze. Micah was stuck in a weird position as if he was almost fully standing but not quite. The white which appeared. Her image blinking in and out like a really bad connection on an old tv. At first, she looked just as she did when she visited me at Reece's apartment; beautiful blonde hair blowing in the wind, a beautiful gown blowing and sweeping the floor. But once she blinked in a third time, the facade was gone. Replaced with filthy rags. Her face was beaten up so badly. She had a black eye, busted lip and she was covered in dried blood and dirt. Her hair was so stiff with dirt and her feet planted on the ground. I tried not to panic but I couldn't understand what was happening.

"I need you... to get out of here.... Alyssa.... is working for the same people that have me." It was so hard to understand her blinking in and out like this.

"I don't understand." Shockingly enough I began to cry because I felt suddenly helpless. Whoever these people were that had the white witch must be ridiculously powerful. Why are they torturing her?

"Blue no tears...right now...I need your strength. Don't underestimate Alyssa... don't underestimate... yourself. I can't hold on much longer... the key to all of this is you.

"How, I'm no one's hero?" I said wiping my own tears.

"You know deep... down that is not true." She was still blinking in and out. "Your blood is ... so special. Your abilities are also special... Alyssa and these people want to use your blood for evil." I gasped. "Blue you...haven't really fed in a while...but look at your ankle." I looked down at it and saw that it was already healed. She was right, a few other vamps talked about how my healing abilities went beyond the vampire norm. But I never thought much of it. "I'm feeling... I'm too weak... your powers...."

"I still don't understand." I begged her to tell me more, but I knew by the air that she was gone and the energy now felt angry and vengeful. Alyssa was on her way.

TRISTAN CHAPTER 20

Something wasn't right. I could feel it. I still haven't heard back from Blue. The meeting was supposed to start in about twenty minutes and her clan was now the only one missing. I texted her hours ago but she never replied. Even though she acted as if I were a nuisance, I could always rely on her replying back to my messages and answering her phone. By now the room was filled with light chatter. The few clans that actually got along seemed happy to be there. Many vampires could not believe a Royal had shown up and kept stealing glances at Tabitha.

Camilla wasn't excited to be here. Her father spoiled her so much. I think up until my alleged sister walked through the door, she thought she was royalty. She felt the way she ran her clan was the best way and she wasn't diplomatic enough to even fake it. I shook my head at the thought when four of Blue's men busted in.

"The USE clan is under attack. We don't know where Blue is." The tall bald guy talking was Tim. He gave off a calm demeanor as he was trained to do but his eyes said otherwise.

He was so scared. I met him once before at Blue's crib. My stomach flopped.

"What the hell do you mean you don't know where Blue is?" I asked while trying my best to not raise my voice. I was ready to strangle him with my bare hands until I felt Camilla's small hand on my shoulder. I took in a deep breath. The room grew silent. Camilla stood; she loves this kind of attention.

"You guys must think we are idiots." She smiled smugly. "Blue didn't have the balls to show up, is that what happened? How pathetic. This is why her clan will never compare to mine." She's smiled at everyone.

"Blue was one of the first female clan leaders in the United States, she basically paved the way for you Camilla." Lolli told her. She didn't get a chance to respond to him. Her cousin Ava stood and spoke up.

"Now wait, I know Blue and she's no coward and she definitely isn't the person who doesn't keep her word. If her men are here and she isn't, then something is up Camilla. I know y'all have issues but this isn't personal, cousin. I say we have to cancel the meeting until Blue is found." The look Camilla gave Ava was enough to kill. Ava slowly slid back down in her seat.

"I second that." Camilla and I had a thirty second stare off but I'm not her cousin. And I damn sure ain't scared her. She better not try and make me pick between them because she will end up heartbroken. I'd choose Blue over anything and anyone.

"Wow." Camilla scoffed. "My own general!"

"Excuse me young and the restless." Zun lee stood up. His pun went over many of the foreigner's heads. "I have traveled for thousands of miles to this godforsaken place, I want to get this meeting over with today."

Chatter erupted around a table. Another clan leader, Abdul of the African clans stood up. "I have known Blue for years she is by far the best leader either US clan has had. He glared at Camilla. She stuck out her chin ready to go at his neck. I slammed my fist down on the table.

"You all have to be kidding me!" I was laughing but the laugh was sinister. I felt like the Joker because at that moment I was in an unstable, uncaring and homicidal mental space.

"Maybe if Blue drank fresh human blood every now and then she would stronger and wouldn't be in this mess. Either way, we cannot hold up a meeting as important as this one for one leader. The VL goes against it," Someone from the royal clan said.

"You think I give a fuck about vampire law right now?" I seethed.

"If I have to go through each and every one of you to get through that door I will." I stared everyone around the table in their eyes with a look so intense. It was the first time Tabitha gave any of this discussion a little of her attention. My chin was up and my shoulders were back, and my fangs were extended. I had already planned my entire attack in my head. Something in my eyes must have told these vampires I wasn't about to play with them or hold back. I needed to get through that door now!

BLUE CHAPTER 21

~~~

Micah finally stood.

"Damn my legs feel tired and cramped that must be a side effect of the white lily." I didn't feel like explaining to him what had just transpired.

"Yeah maybe," I replied. He was totally unaware that he had been standing in a semi-crouched position for about three minutes.

"She's coming, get…" I didn't get to finish my sentence. The doors suddenly exploded. The naturally red headed witch was furious. Her large gray eyes tinted red with fury. She immediately pinned Micah to the wall with her magic.

"You thugs have had power long enough."

Micah and I looked at one another and smirked. We have been called worse. There are many people that hate to see black or brown people have any type of rank or power. But I held my own with the best of them. I am smart, confident, and I was fluent in three languages besides English. I was a very strong black woman with an army behind me. It made people who were prejudice and guilty of ethnocentrism very ruffled, because I couldn't be manipulated or manhandled. One of the reasons I wouldn't allow myself to be with Tristan was because as soon as a powerful woman is associated with a man, everyone acts like the power all came from him. His love made me feel so soft which to any other woman that would be the dream. But I am not your average woman and I couldn't afford that luxury. I understood that now. The witch laughed at me. I gave her a sugary smile. I guess I was enjoying this too much, so with a flick of her wrist, the disgusting cot came flying my way. Okay so we're doing this.

"I guess the weak witch visited you in her desperate attempt for help." Her red hair seemed to laugh along with her and then she threw her head back to laugh. My vampire speed and strength caught her by surprise. I had her by the throat. I easily lifted her off of her feet. Her eyes were wide with shock but only for a second. She flipped her wrist and I felt a very sharp pain shooting up under my ribs. It should've been enough pain for me to let her go but it wasn't, at least not at first. As the pain intensified, I threw Alyssa into the wall. Her head banged against it and she went limp. Micah was let loose from the wall.

"She needs to die," Micah said as he was making his way to the unconscious witch.

"No not like this, it doesn't feel right. I want to kill her with my bare hands while she's staring at me," I jeered as I pulled a short black knife out from under my ribs.

"Damn, okay gangster," Micah said, clearly amused. Suddenly, I watched Micah's eyes widen and then he charged and push me out the way. He was fighting blow for blow with a blonde-haired green-eyed vampire. I remembered Allegra was still locked up. I found her and kicked in the door. She was laying against the wall she was chained to. She was pale and did not look well. I remembered what the white witch told me and decided to go with my gut instinct. I bit my own wrist and placed it at her parched pink lips.

"What the hell Blue? I need human blood." She winced out.

"My blood should help at least heal you." I looked her dead in the eyes and hoped it was true.

"Why should I trust you? I know you and Reece don't like me, especially now after the fight" She spat.

"What fight? Never mind we don't have the time right now. Regardless I can't let you die here. You are only here because you tried to warn me." Her honey brown eyes poured into mine and after a stare off she finally drank.

"I feel amazing!" She jumped up and hugged me. Her high cheekbones beginning to fill with a tiny bit of color.

"Okay so whose ass are we beating first?" She asked me.

"Oh no, I need you to get out of here now! We have this. Trust me!" I told her.

"Maybe you're right. We wouldn't exactly make the best trio," She said as she looked over at Micah who seemed to be avoiding eye contact with us.

"It would be awkward for us all honestly," I told her just as a human guard appeared. She moved super quick as she grabbed one of my knives from out of my pocket knife holder belt.

"This is for Cassie!" She yelled as she charged the guy and stabbed him in the temple. Her attack was a little unorthodox compared to my fighting style but she got the job done. She drank a little from the human before running off without saying another word.

I put my attention back on Micah. I didn't have time to focus on his fight because two large male vampires were coming straight for me. Fighting stance in place, I got mentally prepared. My fighting instructor taught me to look at a fight as if I'm dancing. Let's just say I'm a great dancer. It was nothing for me to end up on top of my class since I was already a fighter as a human.

"Are y'all sure y'all want to do this?" I asked.

The larger of the two men, a tall white male with long black hair that hung past his shoulders swung first. I ducked and dodged it and hit him hard in the face with a right hook. He stumbled back. The next one was on me. He was a large heavyset type with what appeared to be a beer belly. He had red curly hair like Alyssa's. He came in for a grab but he was fat and sloppy.

"Okay, let's dance," I dared.

As he came towards me, I slid to his left and used the corner of the wall to run up a little bit. I jumped up and grabbed the fat neck redhead from behind. I swung both my legs up just in time to kick the fake Fabio in the chest with enough strength to send him crashing into the wall. He collapsed and bits of the wall came crashing down with him. I still had the fat guy around his neck. He was starting to sweat. Gross. I jumped down off of the guy and faced him. He fumbled to take a pocket knife out of his pocket. Okay, no worries. Then three more guys came up behind him and I was getting tired. I held my side for a second but I could not allow myself to feel the pain. I looked back at Micah who had just got punched in the face hard and he went down. He quickly got up, he charged at the guy, slamming him into the floor. Okay so he still busy. Well, time to bring out the big guns. I ran over to the slumped witch and grabbed her wrist and quickly took two big gulps of blood. I was gonna need the energy. Her blood wasn't really good. Definitely O positive type, basic bitch.

TRISTAN CHAPTER 22

Abdul of the African clan was closest to me at the table on my left but I knew he would step to the side. Beside him was Mateo from one of the South American clan. Mateo was a strong, tan, and stocky Latino from Bolivia who glared at me. I could tell by his body language I would probably have the fight him. I looked over at Blue's four men still near the door. Tim gives me a single nod letting me know I will not be fighting on my own.

"Oh fuck," Camilla sucked her teeth. But to my surprise I looked back at her and she was in her fighting stance. My eyes wide with amazement but I quickly got back focused. By now everyone in the conference room was standing up except Tabitha.

"I'll take the left and you and Ava the right," I told Camilla. "I hate her even more now." But I knew she was about to ride it out. Her taser was out but it was all for show. She enjoyed making it seem like she was not an adequate fighter. She was trained to fight before she could even walk. Camilla loved to be underestimated.

"Wait!" Zun Lee interrupted. "the China/India clan doesn't want to fight." I guess he reconsidered.

"Nor does the African tribe," Stated Abdul and they stepped aside. Mateo stepped up.

"If I defeat you in one-on-one combat can the meeting proceed?" Shit. I really didn't have time to deal with this jerk who was still mad about something that happened over fifteen years ago with me and his mom. She was a very sexy woman, but I regret making an enemy over something that was nothing more than a fling.

"Mateo, I don't have time for this, we can fight any time and any place but not right now." I was looking him in his eyes. I saw the rage and anger he wasn't about to let this go. His huge meaty hand slammed down on the table.

"You dishonored my family with your black filth and then expect me to care about some whore." The room gasped. Tim and his men grabbed their guns, clearly feeling disrespected by the comment.

"Racist prick," Ava yelled. He proceeded to unbutton his two small suit jacket. Well, here we go.

"Mateo stop," an attractive, small framed, dark-haired Bolivian woman stepped from behind a very large man. It was Mateo's mom. She was still very beautiful and very powerful. She had the ability to calm you when she talked to you but no one here knew about that ability except myself and the (SAC) South American clan. She was so easy on the eyes, dressed in a red wrap dress, high heels, and huge rocks on her hand.

"This is not the place Mateo." Her red colored lips got close to his ear. I couldn't make out what she said to him but we all watched the fire in his eyes burn out. He began to button up a suit jacket and took a seat.

"This is not over," He told me. Sabrina sashayed back into the shadows. It was so weird, I didn't know she was here in the first place. Looks like Mateo was the only one who really wanted to fight. Everyone else around the table stepped back so I can get through. I started running to the door.

"I'll stay here so we can reschedule this mess," Camilla yelled. I didn't see her face but I knew her eyes were rolling. Blue's guards piled up in the three row black SUV that they took to get here. One of my guards, Chris seemed to be running to the truck and come along too. I tried to tell him to stay but he was one of my closest friends and I guess I could use all the help I could get. Tim's phone started ringing it was Surge.

"Yeah boss?"

BLUE CHAPTER 23

~~~

I used vamp speed to get over to the guard that was across the room. I just needed a little fresh blood. His blood was so warm and inviting, I ended up completely draining him. I needed the energy is what I tried to tell myself. Looking over at Micah, I felt a tinge of worry. If Micah did not make it out of this, I would never be able to look Reece in the eyes again. They were soulmates and I honestly don't believe they would survive living without one another.

I have never seen anyone love as hard as them. Both of them came from horrible backgrounds, where the enemy would have treated them better as children. Reece was absolutely amazing. But no matter how much smarter she was, and how much better at basketball she was than everyone else, her father David, (stepdad technically) would only see her as the black girl he was burdened with. The abuse and treatment she dealt with growing up with David left her with low self-esteem and undoubtedly untrusting of people.

He married her mom when she was only one so David was the only father she knew. Unfortunately, she hardly remembers her mother at all. Reece was only 5 when her mother died. Her death was supposedly suicide but Reece never believed that. The few and far in between memories she did have of her mother, were of them snuggling, baking, and laughing. Her mother's love for her was so deep. Even if she couldn't fully remember certain details clearly, she did remember a feeling. The feeling of being truly, unconditionally loved. It's a feeling that can't be replicated or ever forgotten. Much later Reece found out her mom had gotten pregnant by a free-spirited witch named Relly, who apparently bailed on them unexpectedly, right after Reece was born. David always told her of course he ran off. But she never believed that was the case.

Micah did not come from a fairy tale either. Micah found Reece after escaping his gang banging life when he was left for dead by his own gang members. It was scouts that found Micah and brought him to the Roses. He and I went through bloodlust struggles together in the beginning, but after he got himself under control he became a solider for the clan. Micah and Reece deserve each other and I have to make sure he made it home safely to her.

I went over to Micah's fight and we stood with our backs together just as three more men walked in to the join the fight.

"Let's do it how we did at the night club in Miami." I told him.

"Say less." Micah said as we began to shoot in perfect harmony covering all angles. Micah went high while I went low.

"Damn who taught you how to shoot like that?" He asked jokingly.

"Surge." I told him knowing it ruffled his feathers.

"Damn, I can't never get no credit. But you and I both know the truth. It's the one thing I'm best at!" He said as we began to gather the weapons off of the recently deceased.

TRISTAN CHAPTER 24

"Surge had a gut feeling something was going to happen so he had put a type of tracker in Blue's purse. He figured the ones on the SUV would be taken off or disabled if anything happened and he was right." Tim explained, "Nothing gets past him." They all nodded in agreement.

"Can you drive any faster?" I asked feeling anxious to get there.

"Well, we want to make it there alive so we can help," One of the guards replied as he held on to the handlebar above him. So I guess we were going as fast as we could. I just needed to get my mind off of the current crisis.

"What's up with Surge and Blue anyway?" Blue told me numerous times it was more like a father-daughter relationship than anything else but I still had my moments of jealousy which I usually hid well. Everyone in the truck looked out the window. No one wanted to speak on it. Tim's ball head ass put in his headphones. Well, I guess I shouldn't be mad this is what loyalty looks like.

"I'm just curious," I continued. "It's not often you hear of so many loyal vampires. Especially one as old as Surge being led by a woman a century younger than himself." The driver, a Hispanic guy named Rico spoke up.

"Surge was in charge of all the new recruits that arrived back when King was in charge. He hated it but it was his job. Blue was turned by accident. The recruiter was sent up to find a homeless teenager but Blue happened to be in the wrong alley at the wrong time and rumor has it, the recruiter couldn't resist her. Surge was furious."

"Wait is that how the USE clan got its vampire members?"

"Yea many of them. That is until Blue became our leader," Rico said.

"What the hell? Why?" I looked around at all of them feeling perplexed.

"King was always paranoid that we were so outnumbered by many other clans that we could be easily taken over. He thought everyone he turned would be grateful to him and in return be willing to die again for him if it came down to it. Guess he didn't expect to be overthrown from inside." Rico said as he and another guard fist bumped.

Sounds like everyone appreciated having a clan leader like Blue. King was worse than I thought.

"But anyway, I can't believe I used to work for the asshole." Rico continued "King put no value on female life. Her recruiter almost completely drained her and she was dying. King didn't even blink an eye. So, Surge took her to his apartment and doctored her up and got her back to health. They say it wasn't easy since her cravings were more intense than most freshly turned and sometimes, he had to actually fight her is what I heard. But once they got past that they've been as thick as thieves. No one even spoke to Blue without going to Surge first. He loves her like she was the daughter he never had and protects her like she's the president. The army stuff he was in really messed him up. She's the only person he halfway lets in. When he finds the guys that have her, I don't even want to be in the way. We're 10 minutes away." They all grew silent.

I'm ripping out hearts when I get my hands on these perps but I didn't say it out loud because I'd rather let my actions speak for itself. We finally were pulling up to the property.

"Let me out," I told them. Tim immediately slammed on the breaks.

"I can use my speed to circle the place and find the safest place for us to bust in." They all looked at each other but I didn't have time to wait for permission nor did I care for it. I was about two to three times faster than most other vampires.

I hopped out of the car and slammed the door. I was halfway up the paved driveway in the blink of an eye. I got to the front and after surveying it I decided that the front door will probably not be the smartest way. I was surprised that there weren't any guards outside. I decided left is my first direction I'd check. Suddenly I heard a female voice whisper.

"She needs you now. Go right, use the second door and go straight up the stairs to the third-floor. Go now!"

'*What in the world*' I thought and stopped dead in my tracks I must be losing my mind.

BLUE CHAPTER 25

My bloodlust got the best of me again I realized after I completely drained the guard. I was not happy about it, but now wasn't the time to feel guilty. What scared me was that deep down, in a dark place that I couldn't run to, I knew that I really enjoyed it. Two of the four men were on full attack mode. One of them had been throwing daggers. I was fortunate enough to avoid them, unlike Alyssa who accidentally took one right in the forehead. Damn I was looking forward to killing her myself once she woke up, but looks like that's not going to happen. The accidental killing of one of their own staggered the guy for a second as he stared at Alyssa dumbfounded while I saw an opportunity. I quickly ran over to him and punched him in the face. He went down while another one was making his way over to help his partner fight Micah. The guy he was fighting with was an equal match, add another man in the equation and Micah might be done for. I ran over and blocked his path to Micah. I suddenly heard the white witch whisper in my ear.

"Your powers Blue." The guys were quickly closing in, if I was going to do this, I needed to do this now! I backed up as far as I could and dangerously enough, I closed my eyes. First thing I felt was anger, Micah felt really pissed about still fighting off the same guy for the past twenty minutes. Then I felt shame coming from the fat redhead. I wonder why. And that's when it happened. *'The green group are never going to take me seriously if I can't even kill this skinny twatt.'* He thought

"Skinny twatt?" I laughed. "you don't stand a chance." He turned beet red.

"How did you get in my head bitch?" He charged at me and I simply tripped him and moved to the side to allow him to fall hard. I was breathing heavily, trying to understand what just happened. Did I really just read his thoughts? I've never heard of a vampire being able to read minds before but I did not have time to dwell on it because another big guy was getting up. I went back into the fat guy's mind 'throw yourself over the balcony.' I ordered him without speaking out loud. We're on the third floor so he wouldn't die but he would definitely be hurt. He leaped and fell with a big thud.

The big guy that I had punched came up from behind me and before I had time to react, I felt an intense pain in my ribs. Honestly it was the worst pain I think I've ever felt. He punched me right in my wound. I tried to hold back my scream but this time I couldn't. I blinked back tears and grabbed his face. I faced the short Asian guy and I did a high kick which he partly dodged but I got him a little on the chin. I quickly grabbed his face again. I dug into his eyes sockets until my hands were covered in blood and my fingers could feel his nasal cavity. Whew, what a rush! But suddenly I felt really weak and wobbly. I looked down at my wound and I was losing a lot of blood. This is weird. I looked up and saw everything in threes, I noticed my spilled blood had suddenly caused all fights to cease and all fangs except Micah's were drawn out. It's rare to be a vampire and have other vampires drawn to your blood but I was fully aware that I was one of those rare situations. I'm still not sure why.

"Oh shit!" I heaved.

TRISTAN CHAPTER 26

I must be losing my mind. I continued left until an image of a lady in town rags appeared. Well kind of appeared, she looked more like a hologram blinking in and out.

"Yo, what the hell was in that last pouch of blood?" I said out loud.

"Tristan if you love Blue you will listen to me. Go right now! She doesn't have much time."

"Who the hell are you? Are you the one that sent me that dissolving letter?" I asked.

But the lady was already gone. I looked around. Was I being pranked or something? But for some reason the panicked look on the lady's face made me undoubtedly follow her directions. I got to the door. It wasn't open of course, I had to punch through the glass and reach my hand in and unlock the door. I ran up to the third floor. Micah was knocked out at the top of the stairs. I hope he wasn't dead but I did not have time to check on him because as I walked into the room with the shattered door, I saw her large blue eyes staring straight at me.

"Blue." my words got choked in my throat as I saw her beautiful face distorted with pain from having four vampires feed off of her. She was lying on her back. My stomach twisted in a knot. Her blood was so tantalizing that none of them even looked up at me as I entered. Before I even realize it, I was standing on top of her and the four were vampires dead. I had already broken their necks while they were in a feeding frenzy. All except the guy biting on her throat. I saved him for last. I ripped out his heart out and watched as it pumped those last few beats while outside of his body. Her blood did smell amazing but my mouth didn't even water. I loved this woman more than anything else. The thought of her dying made my eyes mist as I grabbed her limp body into my arms. But she wasn't dead yet. I was about to open my vein up in my wrist when Surge walked in. I didn't even know he was meeting us there.

"No need for that young blood give her this," He handed me a pouch of warm blood.

"No disrespect but due to her injuries Surge I really think she needs fresh blood."

"No Blue wouldn't want that, she doesn't like drinking from people. Just give her the blood, we don't have a lot of time to be talking."

He was right. I ripped the pouch open with my teeth and gently tilted her head back, feeling her braids in my hand. I poured some blood into her mouth. Her eyes look right at me but there was nothing behind them. I think she's in shock. Tim walked over to us and wrapped a blanket around her. I noticed Micah wasn't laying on the stairway anymore. Surge and I made eye contact. We both gave a head nod. Men don't talk much when things get emotional. His commands and body language were relaxed but his eyes gave his true feelings away. He was just as scared that Blue might die.

"I don't get why she isn't healing, it's not like her," Surge said.

"I think I can help." Reese walked in.

"I told you to wait in the car with Micah."

"He woke up and said I better fix Blue or he would burn this whole place down with everyone in it." She looked down as she said it because she knew her husband was not one to give idle threats. Micah thought of Blue as his sister. Blue and Reese were the only thing keeping his crazy ass from becoming a killer rogue vampire.

"Okay, so how can you help?" Surge was talking to her with a cigarette hanging out of the side of his mouth. I think the cigarette was just to keep his mouth and hands busy. Reese knelt down beside us, I still had Blue in my lap. Her hands were shaking as she ran them over Blue's body. I met Reece a few times before. My first impression of her was that she was a cool hippie type. Even with all the talk lately of whether a witch can truly trust a vampire I knew they genuinely loved each other. I trusted Reese because I knew with a best friend like Blue she had to be a good person. Reese pointed one of her extra-long pink nails over towards the dead witch.

"That's our problem the knife or whatever was used a stab her was cursed with a dark spell. It's not allowing the wound to heal. Look at all her bites, they are probably half healed by now." I peeled the gauze back from her neck and Reese was right, it was just about healed up.

"So what now?" I asked. We all looked at one another. Blue started moving on my lap. She started blinking.

"My eyes are so dry," Blue squealed out. We all laughed but it ended quickly because we still weren't in the clear.

BLUE CHAPTER 27

~~~

I was coming to my senses in Tristan's arms and smelling his cologne was enough to make me forget what had just transpired. He had me curled up in his lap, I felt safe. After blinking several times, trying to get my eyes lubricated I noticed many of my guard men, Surge, and Reese were right beside me. I tried to stand.

"Blue wait you aren't healed," Surge said. Tristan was still holding on to me.

"How long have I been down? I should be fine." That's when I felt the sharp pain. It was very achy and unlike anything I was used to.

"What's happening?" I asked. Tristan lifted me up to my feet. Come on we will explain everything on the ride back. I was leaning on Tristan for support when his phone rang. I saw it was Camilla.

"Go ahead and answer it." I don't know why her calling annoyed me so much but I waved my hand dismissing him. Immediately, Tim had my arm around his shoulder helping me to the SUV.

"Blue, let Reese help you change," Surge ordered. "The smell of your blood is too much for it even the most loyal vampires." The rule of the thumb is that vampires don't find other vampires blood appealing. So I'm not sure why my blood is so enticing.

"Okay," I said. Once in the powder room I noticed Reese was surprisingly quiet.

"What's wrong?"

"Nothing let's get you cleaned up." I closed the lid on the toilet and sat down. I was surprised that the water was even still on in this filthy place.

"Why bother lying Reece?" I lifted her chin as she was close to my face washing me off with a cold rag but she never made eye contact. I flinched at the coolness.

"Sorry, only cold water works," she said as she backed away from my hand. I figured I would just let her be. I wasn't the nagging type. She washed all the dried blood off for me. I was almost naked except for my underwear and bra; my dress was in shreds. I noticed all the small scars on my limbs. Damn what a battle. Reece saved the stab wound for last. When she peeled back the gauze, we both gasped. The wound still looked so fresh. It had black veins like marks coming from it and they were spreading outward just a little. She grabbed the first aid kit and that's when I noticed the tears running down her face.

"Reese seriously, what is going on? Since when did we keep secrets?" My voice always remained calm even when I was screaming on the inside. It was one of my gifts. She took a deep breath.

"Remember how I came about finding you guys? I met Micah and he invited me to come stay at the Roses, so I could be with my own kind." She looked down, her painful past usually was not up for conversation.

"Of course I do. The perfect love story." I said, still trying to follow along with her.

"Okay well you know about me being homeless after leaving my prejudiced ass family. But you don't know my mother was considered witch royalty. She was one of the most powerful witches ever. And because of this, she was sanctioned by the royal family. A friend of hers gave me so many pictures of my mom with the royal family." She dug in her shoulder bag and handed me a photo.

"Pay close attention to the girl directly behind Travis of the royal family. Doesn't she look familiar?" She asked me. I just stared at the girl for a moment.

"What does that have to do with today? I don't understand," I questioned as I looked her right in the eyes.

"You know what honestly I'm just tired, it's really nothing," she told me, trying to get off of the subject. But I knew something was bothering her.

I was searching for answers. That's when it hit me. I felt a strong feeling of distress coming off her. We've been through a few battles before so I still was confused because Reese was anything but lily livered. She still wouldn't budge. That's when I took things into my own hands. The white witch said that I was supposed to save something and that I needed to believe in my powers to do so. I closed my eyes just as I did during the fight and inhaled slowly and exhaled even slower. That's when I was in her head. 'There's no doubt in mind that the girl in the picture is closely related to Tristan. I'm worried about him because I'm worried about her. If anything happened to him or if he's a traitor, Blue may not survive it. Red and the others may have saved me from being homeless, but Blue and Micah are who saved me from ME. I can't lose Blue!' And then bam! My head started pounding really hard. When I opened my eyes, I had a migraine and Reese was huge eyed up against the bathroom wall breathing heavy.

"You bitch, you were in my head," She yelled.

"Yeah, I was." I winced pain. "What the heck was that?" Felt like I had hit a brick wall.

"Blue, I know how to block someone out of my head. You only got in because I usually only need to put my blocks up for powerful sorcerers." She threw the wet towel she was holding into the sink. Then she smiled.

"I've never heard of a vampire with this ability Blue. You are the one that the scrolls are talking about." She was looking at me like I was about to stop world hunger and cure cancer.

"So you're worried that Tristan is from the royal family?" I asked

"That and the fact that you are my best friend. My family. You and Micah are literally all I have. The thought of me not being able to fix this is tearing me up, but yes I'm worried about how Tristans truth will affect you" She admitted.

"I'll be fine. But this is just another reason why I chose to stay single," I assured her. I squeezed her hand lightly.

"Okay we've been here long enough," She said as she wiped her tears and helped me up off the toilet. I grabbed the clean clothes quickly and put them on. I got lost in thought. I'm great at running a clan, I'm great at commanding my men, but what if I'm not great at controlling these powers? The world is depending on me and that gives me anxiety. I'm just a clan leader and that's more than enough for me so why was all this happening to me?

TRISTAN CHAPTER 28

~~~

I decided I would stay in the Roses a day or so just to make sure Blue was really okay. I was in deep thought as I walked along the Baltimore harbor. This was a very dangerous city for a vampire that wasn't from here, but I wasn't looking for trouble nor was I worried. There was also something very inviting about the city. The vampire raves here were some of the best I've ever been to and that's saying a lot. I just needed to clear my head with some fresh air.

Everything that just transpired was too much to wrap my mind around. I definitely have feelings for her clearly. I mean look at what I just went through to save her ungrateful ass, but the way she just dismissed me in front of everyone. My fist balled up in frustration. How could she be so cold? The relationship, if you can even call it that, is done. I am an attractive, successful vampire, why the hell should I have to be pressed over someone who clearly isn't interested? I can have anyone I want. Even the sexy owner of the Airbnb I'm staying at flashed her fangs at me.

Besides, for all I know she could be dating Tim or one of her other servants. I said all of this in my head to try to stroke my ego. It wasn't working. I can't keep worrying about Blue. Camilla was super pissed at me for not coming back to the caves and for even leaving in the first place. Apparently, Mateo and I would have to fight sooner or later. I guess when his moms isn't around. I shook my head. Mateo was such a clown and fighting with him will not do anything for me. But I refuse to be disrespected.

Another thing that I have been worried about is what I may or may not have seen at the mansion? Was that lady a ghost? I'm beginning to question my sanity. My head kept going to the image of the lady floating and going in and out of focus. It doesn't make much sense to me. I am a little on the spooked side which sounds crazy considering that I'm an 80-year-old vampire that's visibly stuck at age twenty-two, a forefront in keeping an entire clan safe and I've been in countless fights, but yeah I was spooked.

Something about the whole ordeal made me feel small. Like there was much more going on than just an angry witch with a lover's scorn. I needed to talk to Blue ASAP because It really didn't add up now that I think about it. Why would a witch go through all that trouble and not just kill Blue on site? The cornball Erin was planted in Blue's squad for two months before he even made a move. Blue was very hands on when hiring new guards and even letting people in the Roses. This plan had to have been pre-meditated for months, so someone had to have been doing their homework in order for Erin to even have gotten in. But who?

Blue had beef with many vampires due to her fearlessness. Luckily everyone was in agreement that King was the worst kind of clan leader so no one was mad he was dead, well besides Alyssa. There were people in our community that were upset that she was female and not a natural born vampire. In my opinion it didn't make a vampire any less than. The only difference between natural born vampires and turned vampires was the family secrets and other things like wealth and connections that were passed down. In my opinion, natural borns were just privileged but not everyone thought like me. I felt Blue and I were doing a great job for ourselves as turned vampires. Although after what Tabitha told me, my status is to be discovered.

I guess I kinda understood why some older men were uncomfortable with the whole female leader thing. It was new to the older vampires, foreign almost. But women so far are proving they can lead just as good or better. If Blue and Camilla become allies instead of enemies, they could really do something none of us have ever seen. But worldwide racism would end before that happened. I exhaled deeply. I decided I would shower.

In the shower my mind went into thoughts of my own origin. Did Tabitha's story have any truth to it? How was I a natural born if I was turned by Mr. Brinks? Everything is so uncertain at this point. Where are all my memories? For the life of me I can't remember anything that happened before I turned 22 years old and thinking too hard gave me a migraine. I remember waking up in an infirmary. I don't remember feeling any intense pain all the other vampires talk about. And unlike the Roses, they never send out scouts to look for new vampires because everyone knew they preferred natural born. Which really makes me question my history.

I'm supposedly one of the only turned vampires here. Camilla's dad, Mr. Brinks was still in charge at the time when I arrived. I remember being out at a bar one minute and in an unfamiliar place the next. I always assumed I had just passed out from over drinking even though that had never happened before.

Mr. Brinks had a young face but the wisdom and pain behind his eyes did not match his face. He seemed very eager and welcomed me as if I were a long time friend coming to stay with him. I remember laying in the bed, and he came over to my side and asked me could I fight? I just stared at him. He then explained to me exactly where I was. I didn't believe him at first of course, so he showed me his fangs. But even then, I thought I had been abducted by some crazy lunatics. Then he sent one of the guards to fetch me something to drink. I was parched but I thought nothing of it. I guessed it was from a night of binge drinking. I got down the liquid with a quickness but after too big gulps I realized it was some weird tasting shit. It was so thick.

"What the hell was that?" I asked as I tried to stand.

"Blood," Mr. Brinks had said. Him and all the guards were now laughing. I stumbled back into the bed for a minute. My eyes burned. I looked across the room into the mirror that was on the dresser and I watched as my eyes hazel eyes seem to burn with a new light, making my good looks GQ worthy. I also noticed my image in a mirror looked very faulty like the mirror was moving. A sudden burst of energy was coursing through me and before I could think, I was across the room in a blink of an eye holding my knife to one of the guard's necks. Everyone in the room suddenly looked very serious.

"He's faster than you boss," One of the guards yelled.

"What's going on here. The fuck did y'all do to me?" I was so confused. Mr. Brinks looked over at one of his men.

"Tristan put down the knife. This is your first taste so you have now awakened your true self," Old head said.

"What? Man, I don't even know you. Y'all are crazy I want no parts of this," I was edging my way out the door. Either they were gonna let me out willingly or I was gonna bust out.

"Wait Tristan, answer this one question; how did it taste? Do you want more blood?" He asked me.

"Are you crazy? Hell... no." it came out in a whisper because my body betrayed me. My throat was suddenly feeling raw and I was so dehydrated and I couldn't deny it. I wanted more. I needed it.

BLUE CHAPTER 29

The car ride back was painfully long. I don't think I've ever been in pain like this since I got turn into a vamp. Sunlight doesn't kill us but it's definitely uncomfortable and does burn after a while. Luckily, we arrived at the Roses right as the sun was coming up because my thin wrap dress wasn't much coverage for something like this. Another side effect of the sun is that it makes us weaker; in direct sunlight we have the strength of humans. I heard stories that it wasn't always like this but somehow one of the first humans made a poison and tricked one of the first vampires. It was said to have been created to try and even the playing field.

Once we finally arrived back in the city, I was so anxious to get to bed. I figured I just needed some rest and then I can start to heal. Or that was at least what I was telling myself. One of my guards asked Tristan how he was going to get back to California.

"I will head home from here don't worry about me," Tristan told him. I stepped out of the car thinking I should be fine, but if it wasn't for Surge's strong arms catching me just in the nick of time, I would have fallen flat on my face.

"Everyone get some rest, I will take Blue in," Surge told the guards. Before I could protest, I was completely in the air being carried to the Roses by very strong and large muscular arms. Arms that were strong even in sunlight. Surge's hands were singed by the sun as he ran to the front door holding me on his shoulder.

"You really can put me down now. I'll be fine" I tried to tell him.

"No," he said once we were in the elevator, pushing the fancy go buttons.

"Excuse me? Just because I'm injured doesn't mean..." he cut me off mid-sentence.

"I'm not defying you as second in command, I am defying you as a friend." That shut me up. I actually felt a little misty eyed because I can count on my right hand how many people I trusted and loved, and Surge was definitely number one. He took me in and showed me the ropes when I first arrived here. The love between us was just raw and natural. He was the closest thing to a father I had. Neither one of us was into the mushy stuff though so we never really expressed it.

"Family" was all I could muster out as my eyes closed and I must have passed out before he put me in my bed. When I awakened, my side was still sore but much less than it was when I was in the car. I felt clean and comfortable and I looked under the blanket and noticed that I was in my silk nighty, my bonnet was on and I'm hooked up to some type of IV. I could hear many people in my apartment but I was alone in my room. I heard what sounded like an argument.

"Leave now she isn't up for company like I said already and I won't keep repeating myself." That was Surge, but I'm not sure who he was talking to you.

"Surge, I think we should let him in, it's been three days." That was Reece, her voice was breaking, she was very upset.

"Maybe Tristan can help her wake up." She continued. Oh Tristan was still here? I blushed. Then I felt annoyed. What the hell is he still doing here?

"She will wake up when she is ready. He can't do anything to help her right now," Surge contravened.

"Enough." I didn't yell but I spoke with power that allowed my voice to carry. Surge, Micah, Reece, and Tristan ran in.

"How are you feeling Blue?" It was Reese who asked me but all of them wanted an answer. She grabbed my hand and lightly squeezed it. I slowly slid my hand from her grasp, not particularly fond of this sort of attention. All four of them surrounded my bed and looked at me with relief.

"I'm okay, I feel much better than I did before." I sat up. I felt a little pain but I held back a wince so I wouldn't show it. They all were staring at me looking for a sign that I was in pain.

How long have I been out, did I hear someone say it's been three days?" I questioned.

"Yeah, I had Reece and Vanessa (my house maid) come and put you in the shower." Surge informed me.

"Yeah, and running through your IV is something equivalent to 800 mg Motrin for humans going into your bloodstream to help fight off the pain, and I have been keeping your bandage changed," Reece said.

"You sure are you alright?" Micah asked. He was very tough on the outside but on the inside, he was a teddy bear for the people he loved. Micah and Reece looked at each other and she squeezed his hand. I can tell me being out for the past few days really freaked them out.

"Look at me," I told Micah. He raised his eyes slowly.

"This was not your fault at all," I told him. His eyes teared up and he snatched away from Reese and punch the wall, knocking down one of my priceless artifacts.

"A chill man!" Surge yelled.

"You know damn well it's my fault!" Micah yelled out. I was not surprised by his passion in the least bit. This was Micah we were talking about.

"I was over in the corner getting my ass whooped by one guy while you were fighting like a dozen men alone. You almost died because of me. I'm supposed to protect you!"

Reese ran over and hugged him.

"You heard it straight from the cow's mouth Micah, it was not your fault. If anything, I'm the one that sucks. I'm supposed to be a powerful witch." she throws her hands up dramatically. *Did she just call me a cow?*

"Meanwhile I'm the one that can't even heal my own best friend," Reece continued.

"What the hell is with all the self-blame?" I asked.

"If I could've just gotten there ten minutes sooner. The ghost told me you didn't have much time." Everyone looked at Tristan.

"Okay I'm gonna need all this sadness and self-pity to be put to a stop now." Everyone but Tristan nodded. All eyes are on him again. Reece and Micah got themselves together and were back surrounding my bed with Surge and Tristan. I glared at Tristan, my eyes turned into deadly slits. He didn't realize with a one-word command Surge or Micah would slit his throat and not even think about it.

"This is awkward but...well to be honest I don't work for you." He rubbed his hand on the back of his head, over his perfect red waves. His smile was breathtaking. Focus Blue I told myself.

"While you're in my coven, my rules are law. Matter fact why are you still in my coven? And what did you mean a witch told you I didn't have much time?" He looked uncomfortable for the first time ever. Before we could get to the bottom of this Rico, one of my guards busted in.

"Surge there has been another attack on a vampire coven. His eyes were big he was trying to remain calm but it wasn't really working.

"Come in Rico I'm awake."

TRISTAN CHAPTER 30

I can't believe Blue has been out for three days. My stomach felt sick the whole time. The dark magic is more powerful than we thought. At least a half of dozen witches have come to see the wound and see if there was anything they could do. So far everyone felt stumped. I've been stopping by her crib every day since I've been here, but today I wanted to actually lay my eyes on her. I knew the guys will give me a hard time. It didn't make any difference to me. My mind was set on seeing her. When I heard her voice command, something inside my heart raced a little with joy. When did I get so soft? Now as we were all by her bedside one of her body guard's burst in with more bad news. I was so sure they were going to throw me out since I wasn't in the clan. But to my surprise Blue allowed me to stay.

"So which coven got hit?" I asked the guard. He just stared at me for a second until Blue gently nodded.

"The Central Europe clan. They killed about five of them but unlike the cold ones they were not as unprepared and they fought back. They also had a few powerful witches in their clan which was great because the rumors are true, this enemy does possess some sort of magical power. They captured one of the intruders," He informed us. Everyone gasped.

"That's not all boss," he looked at Blue "the captive is human."

"Oh my God!" Reese cried out because this was way worse. It was starting to feel like a nightmare. Humans greatly outnumber vampires. Yes, we were stronger and faster but if they were capturing us, they must be outthinking us and it's just a matter of time before they found out our weaknesses. We all grew silent thinking about it all. My phone beeped. I had five missed calls from Camilla.

"I'll be right back." I tried to walk out before I answered, for good reason. Camilla never had a filter.

"I hope you lovebirds are doing better because I need you here now!" She hung up. I didn't even get a word in. *Well damn.* I went back inside. I couldn't leave without speaking to Blue about what's been going on and try to make sense of why that witch Alyssa went through all that trouble.

I was just about to head back into her room but when I went to reach for her door, one of the guards stopped me and wouldn't let me in. He informed me that she was getting dressed and now that I knew she was doing okay I should return to the caves. So much for Baltimore hospitality. I scoffed, walked off but of course I didn't listen. I wasn't done here. Blue's attack wasn't making any sense and I couldn't believe I was the only one trying to get to the bottom of it all. I decided to pay someone a visit. The one person who cared about Blue just as much as I did.

Surge answered the door before I could even get to the second knock. I realized I needed a great mind, and most importantly someone Blue trusted. He was shirtless, had huge arms and a massive chest but he didn't look like his normal self. He let me right in which was ridiculously shocking. It was no secret that this man didn't care for me, so for him to just let me into his home was a bit unexpected.

His apartment is so simple with hardly any décor, especially compared to Camellias or Blues penthouses or even my flashy man cave. He had one brown couch and one brown recliner that looked like his go to seat. There was a huge husky staring at me as I walked in. He was so silent. I didn't even notice him at first which was really upsetting to my ego. Surge yelled out something in what I think was German and the dog ran and went into one of the bedrooms. I wish we could have dogs at the caves.

"I know why you're here Tristan, have a seat. I don't want to break my train of thought so let me just finish reading this article right quick." I hated being bossed around. I remain standing, my eyebrows raised. He continued pacing around while reading something, he was deep in thought. I was very interested in what he thought was my reason for being here.

There were open books and scrolls everywhere on the countertops and on the coffee table.

As I got closer to one scroll it read the legend of the blue-eyed guardian. I picked it up and skimmed it. It spoke of a one day a great war would come and what would happen if it was not stopped by the guardian whose heart was fair and true. I noticed Surge had finally stopped his pacing and was staring at me.

"You can read that?" He asked, staring at me intently. I didn't even pay it any mind that it wasn't in English.

"How is that possible? This scroll is written in ancient vampire dialect. Only a natural born vampire should be able to read it." I dropped the scroll.

"About that…" I felt a little dizzy. Something wasn't making sense. Suddenly I felt the hot heat coming from behind me.

"What the… " I looked over at Surge and he was just as bewildered as I was. Floating before us was a lady with dirty blonde hair and a dirty face wearing torn rags. She appeared to be blinking in and out. What the hell happened to this ghost lady? The last time I saw her she was clean and pristine looking.

"You two… Are on the right track… Tristan… Natural… Surge Help… Guide Blue I must go… Find me… Only I can save." Then she was gone we looked at each other.

The Baltimore clan

"Yo, tell me I'm not losing it and that you see her too?" I asked Surge.

"Yeah." was all he said I believe he was having trouble digesting it all.

"Well good because that's one thing I came here to talk to you about," I told him. We began discussing everything. I told him all about Tabitha, which felt like a weight was being lifted off my shoulders since I haven't trusted anyone else enough to share that information. This conversation continued for about three hours. I even mentioned to him that it wasn't my first time seeing her and that I received a letter from the witch too. Surge then filled me in on the different legends he has heard throughout the years. Apparently, they have always been intriguing to him.

Surge's penthouse was directly across from Blues, but they were massive. Even though they were huge we were still able to hear yelling from across the hall. The screams sounded like Blue and Micah. Which means they were loud. We looked at each other and both jumped up. Blue's guards were all holding their positions, looking very confused since she was arguing with her third in command, they did not know what to do. Both Micah and Blue were technically their boss.

BLUE CHAPTER 31

After I finally got dressed, I sent a guard to find the elder witch, Red. She was the oldest witch here, she was Reese's mentor and she's one someone I trusted. If anyone here could help explain the white witch and dark magic that was stopping me from healing it would be her. She arrived within fifteen minutes which wasn't surprising since she lived here in the Roses. She was a small framed Native American. Her grey highlighted jet black hair was hanging past her butt and she still wore beautiful Native American pieces. She walked in with the assistance of a cane which was concerning because just a few weeks ago she was fine.

"How are you Red? I heard the funeral was lovely, sorry I was unable to make it."

"It was beautiful, her spirit smiled. Unfortunately, that is the only good news I bring today. I fear that the clan attacks, your attack, and the missing white witch are all tied together," She said through gently wrinkled lips.

"Wait, what do you mean the white witch is missing?" I asked Red. She looked very tired. She looked me in my eyes.

"Alex came to me in my dreams. She is being held captive and is being tortured and experimented on. She looks so sad," she told me. I felt heartbroken and I suddenly began to understand.

Witches don't die naturally but once they hit a certain age, they become tired, weak, and uncomfortable. But before that happens, usually the white witch comes and relieves them. Alex already came to Red but cannot send her spirit into the next life because she was being held captive.

"I'm supposed to be already gone from this body but until Alex is freed, I'm stuck here," She said with eyes of sorrow.

"The wounds that have been inflicted on you can only be healed by Alex. No one else on the good side is powerful enough. Not even me. But I can give you a little bit of temporary relief, then you must hurry and find Alexandria. Reese come, I'm going to need your strength." She motioned Reece over. They laid four hands on my wound as I laid on my couch. They chanted a Latin spell and a few minutes later I could sit up with almost zero pain.

"Thank you so much Red, and you too Reece. I want you to put her in the empty guest suite. Give her anything she needs." I motioned to the guards, who were keeping their distance, to come on in with my hands.

"Of course." Tim nodded and showed Red the way to one of my best suites. She paused. At that moment I was staring at a Red speechless. Her strength and loyalty reminded me of someone, my mom perhaps. Her eyes watered and I had to turn around quickly because I did not want her to see the tears that were falling from my eyes. After a few seconds, I got myself together. Reese accompanied Red out. I gathered many weapons from my weapon room. This room was my favorite place in the house. It was a small room about the size of a large walk-in closet. One wall consisted of all different varieties of guns and then on the opposite wall I had my knife collection. I also have a bulletproof vest, poisoned arrows, and throwing stars all organized by category. Micah walked in. I wasn't expecting him.

"Reese told me about the new mission. When are we leaving and you called Surge?" I turned around to face him.

"What? There is no we," I said calmly but, in my head, I was screaming. I took a deep breath and regained composure.

"I'm not putting anyone else in any more danger I'm going to on this mission alone." I was done with the conversation so I turned back around to finish picking up my weapons. I grabbed two Glock 17s and put them in a holster on my waist. I securely placed my inner thigh knife strap and began throwing some more stuff in my Gucci backpack.

Things like flares, bullets, an MP5, a first aid kit, and some blood pouches.

"I love you Blue but nah, I ain't feeling this." He threw his shoulders back and stared right into my eyes.

"I can handle myself and we both already know that." That was a low blow for me but I did not have time to argue. He acted like the comment rolled off his back but I knew better.

"I'm not about to be here arguing with you, you know that's not me," He told me with his head lifted.

"I said what I said!" I told him shaking my head while placing my favorite knife in its strap on my thigh.

"The crazy part is Blue, yea you might be a better fighter than me. Cool! But you also got me fucked up if you think I'm going to let your overconfident, I don't need a man having ass walk out of here by yourself." He did the dramatics with his hands as he said all this. He wasn't one to hold back his tongue and neither was I. I also knew I didn't have time to stand around with him all day. Red said I was on borrowed time with my wound.

"Okay Micah you're right. I do feel like I don't need a man because anything I want or need, I can get it on my own." I approached him and noticed the considerable difference between now and normally being in heels. We usually are more eye level with each other. Since I was wearing my fuzzy white slippers, I had to look up at him. I got right up under his chin and grab his face roughly. He didn't resist; his eyes just burned with fury.

"If you would have actually taken your training seriously like everybody else here you wouldn't have gotten your ass handed to you like you did the other day." He shook his face outta my grasp.

"Everybody needs somebody Blue. Your ass wouldn't even be on that damn high horse if it wasn't for me, Reece and Surge. So what are you saying?" He was known for hyper behavior once he was upset. He counted off his fingers as he yelled. The statement ruffled my feathers more than it should have.

"So wait you feel like I owe y'all something?" I crinkled my nose up in disbelief. I've never doubted that I needed help to get to where I am but I need him to respect and understand that I'm a force to reckon with either way.

"I stand on my own two feet Micah and you know that, wow." I scoffed. "Such a typical man."

"And you're such a typical female, can't even admit when you need help. Just so you can come back in a body bag. I'm not doing this Blue, I'm going!" He was yelling at this point. Before it could get any further, Surge and Tristan walked in. Surge gave us both the same look. The look a father would give his teenage siblings because that's where we were acting like.

"We have a way more concerning issues than to be fighting with each other," Surge stated. I know better than this shit. I held my head down slightly, out of self-disappointment. Even though we love each other like siblings we shouldn't be arguing as such. I was the leader of the best vampire clan ever for crying out loud.

TRISTAN CHAPTER 32

~~~

We arrived at Blue's crib just in time to break them up. They were really going at it when we walked in. I look at Blue and she looked away. This is the first time I've seen her out of character. I think it was all the stress that was getting to her.

"We will accompany Blue on the trip Micah. The witch told us we were on the right track. Saving her will save Blue," Surge said.

"And apparently saving Blue will save the world," I said.

"Wait, a white witch?" Micah asked looking so lost. I knew the feeling. I was still trying to wrap my mind around all of this. We explained everything we just recently found out to Micah and Blue. Starting with the fact that we believed Alyssa was working with humans.

"The green group," Blue whispered. We all looked at her, waiting for her to continue.

"Yeah," she began "when I was in Alyssa's brother's head, he said something about a green group." I pulled out my iPhone to see if anything popped up if I did a search. Sure

The Baltimore clan

enough, the green group was an organization in the middle of Colorado. Their mission statement was; *Making sure our children's children have a fair chance in living life to the fullest.* Underneath that, it stated *Human and in charge.* Apparently, this group was afraid to be anything less than the top of the food chain.

"Wait a minute Blue, what do you mean in his mind?" Surge question her pulling out a cigarette.

"Don't light that in here," She told Surge.

"Okay, now back to the question," He said.

"Oh yeah." Her fingers tapping her leg very slightly, something I just recently noticed she does when she felt anxious.

"I can kind of read minds if I really focus. I'm not really hundred percent sure how it all works yet. I've only done it twice so can we just get a move on?" She tried to change the subject again but it wasn't going to work. I stared at her. We all stared at her in shock. We were all in pretty close proximity to her gun closet.

"Oh yeah, and I kind of read Reese's mind," She said quickly.

"Boss you can't just read people's minds! That's crazy! Damn did you see us having sex? Is anyone's mind safe?" Micah was going at it again. Getting all worked up and angry.

"What the hell? No! I only pried long enough to try and figure out what was bothering her. She was acting so distant, which isn't like her." Blue said. She really looks sorry. I hate to see this look on her face. I put a reassuring hand on her shoulder, she lets it sit for like three seconds and then removed it. Why the hell do I bother? I asked myself.

"You do know the world doesn't actually revolve are you right?" Micah screamed. Blue was no longer was even facing him. She continued packing her backpack with weapons. I just realized I'd never been in here before. I took a second to take it all in. It was marvelous.

"Like I said" Surge began, "Micah we all get your point. We need to focus on getting…" he shook his hand loosely at Blue for a reminder of what the group was called.

"The green group," Blue replied, tucking yet another knife into her pants.

"Blue are you sure you can travel?" Am I the only one who didn't forget that she literally just woke up from a coma?

"Yes, and I'm on a short time though, so we need to leave tonight. Shouldn't you be back at the caves by now?" Her eyebrows raised.

"This is more important. We also found out that those blue eyes of yours were talked about since the beginning of time. They called you the soul reader. Along with many other names," I explained to her.

"Well let's slow down a minute, how can we be sure it's me?" She asked.

"Look around Blue. I don't see any other blue-eyed black vampires with mind reading abilities," Surge told her.

"Well, it's a lot for one person," She mumbled.

"Look around again. We just almost had to physically throw Micah's scary ass out of here because he didn't want you to go alone. Blue you are never alone." She looked at me then Micah.

"Yea I don't know about all that." He stared intensely for a second then cracked a smile. Micah and I had the same sense of humor.

"And I'm always here if you would just let me be." I reached out and grabbed her hand. I know this must be awkward for Surge but I had to let her know.

"Okay so just so we are all on the same page; I'm a blue-eyed mind reading vampire that must find the most powerful witch in the world, rescue her from a human organization whose main goal in life is to annihilate anybody that isn't human, did I miss anything?" Blue said as she put her backpack on. We were all headed out the door when Reece walked in.

"Blue I think you come from witch descent," Reece blurt out.

"Yeah, and I think I may be a natural born vampire," I blurted out too.

"What? She took her backpack off. Okay I think a need a drink. Anyone else?" Blue asked. We all ended up with a stiff drink. Reece and Blue sat next to each other at Blue's table. The guys remained standing. Reece began to fill us all in on her new findings.

"Okay, so you know that old musty book your mom gave you when she passed?" Reece asked Blue.

"Yea, and I asked you if you knew anything about it years ago and you told me no," Blue replied her eyes narrowing in on everyone's face. Probably looking to see if anyone else was already knowledgeable about whatever it was that Reece found out.

"Yea and I was being honest. But when you got sick, I was putting your things away when I noticed it." She held up the old book.

"This symbol was not here when you first showed me this book."

"What the hell?" Blue gasped. "That definitely was not there before."

"Actually, I think it was, but it only revealed itself once you went into a coma. Blue…" Reece placed a hand on Blue's knee.

"The only reason you are alive is because the spelled knife turned on your witch powers. And that's not all, look." She opened the book and it was filled with spells or something. The book looked oddly familiar to me.

"What, witch powers? This is insane. My mom was definitely human." Blue's jaw suddenly dropped. "So, my dad must be…" She didn't finish her sentence. She did not have to. Her dad was a warlock. That makes the fact that he abandoned her worse.

"Okay enough about me. Tristan didn't you blurt out crazy news as well?" Blue said. They all looked at me.

"Yeah, apparently I can read the ancient language even though I've never seen it before a day in my life. And my story of how I came to be a vampire has always been shaky." I told them. I noticed the tiniest of nods between Blue and Reece. I could hear Reece let out a deep breath. Something tells me they already knew something of that nature.

"Yes, like how you didn't feel like your skin was being burned over and over again when you first got turned," Blue said.

"Wow this day is full of surprises." She turned her attention to Micah.

"You're in charge of the clan while we are all away Micah, you think you can handle that for a few days?" His anger retracted just a little bit.

"Yeah of course I can handle it. Y'all be safe." After Surge, Blue and myself left, he and Reece hugged each other so tight. Their love could be felt for each other even when they were sitting across the room from one another. *One day I will have that* I thought to myself.

BLUE CHAPTER 33

We loaded up the SUV after we had the correct address for the green group and headed out. I was a little nervous about the trip. It wasn't like our normal rides where we would get a fancy hotel halfway through, to sleep, eat and avoid the sun or hop on a private plane and get to our destination in no time. We didn't have that luxury today. I really wanted to know more about the book but Reece needed to stay behind to help Micah keep the coven safe.

Tim insisted on coming with us to help drive and offer his first aid skills. Tim was a certified nursing assistant before he was turned into a vampire. He was perfectly fine around blood spill, which was more than I can say for most of my men or women. Even the witches and the few humans I had in the coven trusted him. I have a lot of respect for him because whenever anyone needed help in our infirmary, he's the first to volunteer. He was as good on the field as he was in a hospital setting. I'm surprised he isn't married.

I automatically hopped in the back, Tim drove first, Surge called shotgun, and you guessed it, Tristan was in the back with me. The ride started off silent at first. I kind of stared at the back of Surge's bald head as a distraction.

The Roses was a magical place to me. I've been here 52 years but still to this day I love the way the water bounced off of the harbor. The witches that designed this were talented to say the least and ahead of their time. The ride was silent for about the first half an hour then Tim finally broke the silence by asking Tristan about Camilla. I tuned out for as long as I could.

"So, is she single?" he questioned Tristan.

"Yeah but I don't think she's your type man," Tristan told him.

"Damn what makes you say that?" Tim asked Tristan.

"She's just a lot to handle is what I mean."

"Damn so are you handling her? Because I thought you were busy enough with the boss," Tim said, immediately regretting it.

Surge glared at him. The stare was deadly. It was as if he wanted to tell Tim to pull the truck over so he could whoop his ass himself.

"Disrespect Blue's name again and you'll be doctoring up your own damn tongue that I cut out of your mouth," Surge warned. Tim swallowed. Surge could be scarier than your worst nightmare when he got pissed.

"No, I didn't mean no disrespect, I just didn't know Camilla was off-limits," Tim said through pressed lips.

"She isn't seeing anyone to my knowledge. She certainly isn't seeing me." Tristan stated, looking very bored with it all. I told myself it was none of my business but I still somehow heard myself talking.

"But you know she wants to be with you," I said.

"We've already established boundaries in which we do not cross years ago Blue and you know that. Don't play with me," I told her. Him and Surge stared at each other. So much testosterone in here.

"Whatever you say Tristan," I rolled my eyes trying to brush off the deep feeling of loss and put my headphones in. My playlist consisted of all R&B, especially 90's R&B. But I was in the mood for something else. I decided on some Wale. His smooth poetic raps usually had a way of making me feel like a sexy black queen.

I must've fallen asleep because the next thing I knew, we pulled over at a Quick Mart to get some gas. Surge was switching seats with Tim. It was now his turn to drive.

"We are making great time Blue, how are you feeling?" He asked, looking at me in the rear-view mirror, his brow wrinkled with concern.

"I'm fine. I'm going to use the restroom real quick." I hopped out of the SUV a little too quickly and I immediately noticed that the pain was increasing in my wound. It was still bearable so I was fine for now, just moderately uncomfortable.

"She bites the bullet better than anyone I've ever met." I heard Surge tell Tim.

"I know right," Tim said in agreement. Tristan got out on his side. Some kids darted out in front him.

"Don't eat that Kells! Do you want to catch corona virus?" The older boy said to the little girl. The seriousness in the little boys voice was pretty cute. I caught Tristan watching the children and smiling. After my bathroom break I hopped back in the truck and there were some blood pouches waiting on my seat. My phone rang it was Micah.

"What's going on Micah?" I asked.

"I may have underestimated this situation. You need to be very careful, these humans are treacherous," He explained. Reece grabbed the phone.

"They are dangerous girl," She roared. Micah grabbed the phone back.

"Also, we just found out that three members of the our clan got into the white Lily drug. Apparently, they got so high that they tried to attack several humans at a nightclub in Fells

Point but luckily we were able to take them out. Don't worry Blue we handled it before there was too much of a scene."

"Okay y'all no worries, I trust y'all can continue to handle it," I told them before hanging up. But still, I was fuming over the fact that this drug has now reached my home.

TRISTAN CHAPTER 34

~~~

Blue must be crazy if she thinks I didn't notice her increased discomfort. As soon as she woke up, I noticed but being Blue she tried to hide it. *Why am I so connected with her?* I asked myself. I was glad we were all distracted enough that I didn't have to talk about my own newly found information about me being a natural born vampire and all. It really didn't change anything but at the same time, it changed everything. Some aspects of it made a lot of sense, like my speed. Even my acceptance into the Cali clan. I've always found it odd that they clearly look down upon vampires that weren't naturally born but yet they always treated me as equal from day one. Camilla's dad was always thought to be biased against anything that wasn't what his family called pure. Luckily, he was politically smart enough not to express it too much or allow it to get in the way of business, but deep down that is how they all felt. But I will say with each new generation it seems to be letting up just a little bit.

I looked over at Blue, she had her headphones back in. This was the first time I've ever seen her in jeans and a T-shirt and chucks and she looked marvelous. I didn't even know she owned those things. She was swinging her head from side to side. I'm not sure what she was listening to. As I continue staring, she looked at me. Her eyes poured into my soul, suddenly I got the weirdest feeling like my brain was suddenly too big for my head. My thoughts went back to the funny kids that ran into the store before Blue and I. If what Tabitha said was true then technically I could have children. But it would have to be with a turned vampire. Where would that leave Blue?

"Blue stop!" I barked.

"What's going on?" Surge was asking from the front seat.

"I'm sorry," She said as she looked him straight in the eyes then diverted her eyes out the window.

"You are trippin Blue. If you want to know something about me dammit just asked me," I said seething through gritted teeth. Because she already knew that. The truth was, Blue didn't want to ask because she didn't want to seem like she cared. She was fighting the truth within herself and only she could wake up and smell the coffee.

It was quiet for like an hour. The sun was rising so everyone was trying to fight against our nocturnal nature and fought to stay awake. I grab the energy drink out of the cooler and told Surge to pull over, it was now my time to drive. We were in Illinois; about halfway there, we still had about fifteen more hours to go. I threw my drink back. Inside our UV ray blocking SUV, we were pretty much fine.

I looked back at Blue who was sound asleep. I noticed Surge staring at her and I knew that he was checking her breathing to make sure she was stable. He must've been satisfied because he sat back in his seat in front of me and was asleep within a minute. He must be exhausted to go out so fast.

"Do those energy drinks really work?" Tim asked, leaning back from his seat.

"Yeah they do, they just wear off quickly. Try one. I grabbed plenty of them," I told him.

BLUE CHAPTER 35

~~~

What the hell was I thinking trying to get into Tristan's head like that? I don't know what I'm doing with this mind reading thing and even if I did, why would I care about what's in his mind? I wondered. Deep down I knew I was trying to convince myself that I didn't know that I loved this man since our first date. It was so simple, yet charming. I just woke up but suddenly it felt like I haven't rested in months. My wound ached deeply. I looked up and literally three sets of eyeballs were on me. I hope I didn't look like how I felt.

"What are you guys looking at? I'm fine," I said through an attempted deadpan expression.

"Damn what do you take us for Blue, idiots?" Tristan was looking at me like he was getting fed up. But they were right and it was taking a lot of my energy trying to keep up the act like everything was fine.

"You don't have to act like you're not in pain for us to still see you as our leader. The wound you've been afflicted with is not your average wound and it looks like your attempts to read minds takes even more of your strength." Surge was attempting to look at me empathetically but all I saw was pity.

"I don't need you guys to feel sorry for me. I have a high tolerance for pain. I said I'm fine y'all should respect that," I said, suddenly stirred up with anger. How can I allow myself to be set up in such a stupid situation? What kind of leader can't even keep her clan safe? My eyes suddenly burned. I better not cry. I would not cry. I turned my chin up and looked out the window before my softness was discovered. A hand was gently placed on my shoulder.

"You are the best clan leader who ever lived. Not only are you just as tough as any man I know, but you are strategic and brilliant. There is no one I'd rather follow even into the pits of hell than you. But you have to take it easy if we don't find the white witch in time Blue, you will die. Get some rest." Surge concluded. Truth be told I was too tired to even argue. I closed my eyes just as he and Tristan were switching seats. We would be arriving in Colorado in just a few more hours.

I closed my eyes for what felt like a second, but I must be dreaming because when I opened my eyes, I was no longer in my luxury SUV. I was in what appeared to be the back of a carriage.

"We are almost here my love. Get prepared," The guy driving the carriage yelled back.

"Tristan?" I asked. This guy looked almost identical to Tristan but his face was a lot squarer. His red hair hung long down his back, he was still handsome. Where the hell was I?

"What's going on?" I asked. "And did you just call me my love? You know we haven't been like that in a while." I noticed I was in a huge ridiculous dress. And my voice was so much lighter. I hated all of this.

"Are you sure you are up for this my love?" The strange guy asked me again. "You know if we don't defeat this giant, no one will Sherry." He looked so concerned.

"Defeat what…?" before I could get my sentence out, I was being thrust into the air from the carriage. I fell very hard into some shrubs. I lay there for a second trying to get myself together. I wasn't sure what kind of place this was but dream or not I'm gonna fuck this giant up!

"SHERRY! CATCH!" Tristan threw my old musty book with the red pages at me.

"What the hell am I supposed to do with this. Who the hell is Sherry?" I'm not sure what, but something made me open the book and look through it. I fully understood the spells. How is this possible? The book opened and a spell for destroying a giant was right in my face. Okay, this is insane but let's do this. I told myself. I ran over to the guy that looked like Tristan. He looked like he could use a hand. The Giant was playing whack a mole with him. I grabbed the sword from around his waist and ran around behind the giant while he was distracted. I sliced through the back of his ankle, making the cut as long as the sword itself. Almost totally amputating it. The giant stumbled back.

"You bitch!" The giant yelled. I was taken aback that he could talk and got distracted. The Tristan look-alike knocked me out of the way just in time. The club struck him and he was lying face down in the dirt.

"Oh no!" I said. I need to finish this now. With sword in hand, I climbed the tree while the giant was still distracted and trying to wrap something around his ankle to stop the bleeding. They weren't as dumb as I'd expect, I told myself. I reach the top of the tree and without even thinking of it, I leaped down and struck the giant right in his eye as I recited the spell. The giant fell with the loudest of thuds. His eyeball sizzled and the scent was horrible to the nostrils. What kind of vivid dream is this?

I ran over to the guy. He had turned himself over and was trying to sit up but his left leg was completely pulverized and his head bled profusely.

"Why did you save me? I asked fighting back tears. I don't know why, but this guy really reminded me of Tristan and to see him in this pain was almost unbearable.

"You are the love of my life Sherry. In this life and the next. Under this moon, or another I will always find you." He told me. He tried to laugh but began to cough.

"Okay I'm just gonna close my eyes. But you should head home. The dogs will be worried about us if you don't make it home before dark." I don't know how but I knew he was talking about our two Great Pyrenees dogs Milo and Sophie.

"You know me," He croaked. "You know it takes a lot more than a giant to get rid of the mighty Shiraz." He had the same sense of humor as Tristan. I began sobbing in his arms, he held me close. If this is a dream, why am I overwhelmed with sadness and grief? I slept the remaining hours and I woke up to Tristan and Surge both saying my name. Surge was gently nudging me.

"We've been trying to wake you for about ten minutes. We're re here," said Surge. The look of wariness in their eyes was enough to make me nauseous. "

I don't know if she will be able to do the mission." Tristan sounded as if his voice was cracking on him. Such a long way from his normal self-assured personality. We were pulled over into an empty parking lot in the middle of nowhere. I felt as if I've been hit by a truck and there was no faking that. I felt a very warm breeze suddenly. Tim dropped the pouch of blood he was drinking as we watched Alexandria blink in and out and try to communicate with us.

"Blue... I don't have much strength... Humans are expecting you... Set up... You guys... Need a new plan... Please." I was having trouble focusing but I definitely heard the word set up. The witch's hologram came back into view and she was crying now.

"Please help me..." Was all she said then it appeared someone hit her hard in the back of the head and then we were just left with the darkness. We quickly pulled out of the vacant lot on three wheels. Suddenly something hit the roof of the truck with a loud bang.

"I got it." Surge yelled as he hung out of the window and began shooting. We looked over to the underground entrance we were just planning on using. How the hell did they all set us up like this? Suddenly the person that was on the roof was right beside my window. Flying next to the SUV! She was beautiful, but clearly pissed.

"Is she the one that has you whipped? She's not even all that!" Crystal yelled in between throwing fire balls. Then suddenly she began to fly back in the direction of the entrance.

"She's bad as hell, ain't no denying that." Tristan told her without thinking. I passed out again.

TRISTAN CHAPTER 36

We pulled off on three wheels. I looked back just in time to see Crystals crazy ass throw a fire ball at the SUV. She threw her voice somehow and we heard her clear as day as if she were in the truck with us.

"Tristan you ungrateful son of a bitch!" Her voice echoed and I was so relieved that Blue slept through it all. I could feel Surge big ass glaring at me.

"And what was that bout motherfucker? We cool but you know I'll mess you up over that one" He asked me as he pointed to Blue in the back seat.

"Just some witch I hung with one time but decided she was to crazy for me." I told them as Tim looked unconvinced and rolled his eyes. Surge did not say anything he just grunted.

"Only top level witches can manipulate gravity and fly like that. Did you know she was a top level witch before you pissed her off?" Tim asked.

"She wasn't, it must be the drugs the human are giving their henchmen." I told them feeling annoyed that Crystal really could of hurt Blue.

If the witch did not warn us about the human setup, we most likely would be dead. At least I know I would've, because I'd rather die than let anybody harm Blue. I looked back over at her and she definitely looked as though she couldn't take any bullets or even hits right now. I had to find a way to save her. It was up to me because she was too stubborn. I'm not underestimating Surge at all, but I know he would go all out for Blue without giving it a second thought because of pure love. And to think humans believe vampires are incapable of love. I snorted at the thought. My phone rang, it was one of my men from the Cali clan.

"Hello"

"Hello, it's Charles." His voice sounded grave.

"What's going on?" I was in the passenger seat. I sat straight up and lean right close to the door. I don't need her in my business. We have been attacked. We lost about five soldiers. They snuck up on us during the day and were trying to disable our sun blocking system. We gave it everything we had but if it wasn't for the bunker, we would all be dead.

"Is Camilla safe?" I heard rustling in the back, sure enough, they were all listening now.

"She's fine. You know she was the first one in the bunker." He tried to joke but something was eating him up. I remember his brother was on the first line of defense.

"Who did we lose Charles?"

"Eddie, Ronald, Kim, Lewis and…" His voice croaked out

"Kristof." I let the silence linger for about five seconds. I didn't know what it felt like to lose a sibling but I know the two of them were as thick as thieves. Oddly enough conversations like this really make me angry when I remember I don't have normal childhood memories or any memories before arriving at the caves.

"He will have a proper going away ceremony as soon as I return." I assured him.

"Thank you, sir." There's enough food in the bunker to last for six months but I should be back in a few days.

"How did they know the entire layout of our place sir?" He asked me.

"It had to be the humans, they have the great books from the cold ones clan. We will discuss it more when I return.

"Okay sir."

"Go down into the bunker until I arrive, get a headcount and stay safe."

"You do the same." As soon as I hung up Blue asked, "What's going on?" She sounded extremely weak.

"We are about to pull over and we will make a new game plan before we go any further. I told them. I pointed to the boulder and Tim pulled over on the side of a country road in Kansas. There was a beautiful chalky cliff that we all walked over to. Blue took her time but her face lit up when she noticed how breathtaking the view was. I think the fresh air did something good for her. The moonlight bounced of her chocolate skin; her eyes shimmered. How can she be so weak and still be so attractive? I thought to myself. We all stood on the cliff's edge, mesmerized by the view. Surge was the first to speak up.

"We were so close to being ambushed." He began to pace.

"And how do we know we can trust the white witch and what could these humans want?" Blue sat down heavily.

"We can trust her; you'll just have to trust me on that. And I'm not sure what they want but with humans, it's usually power. They feel threatened by our strengths. All we need to concern ourselves with now is staying alive and keeping our clans safe." Our eyes met. We continued to discuss new options for a new plan of attack to free the white witch and restore balance.

"Before we can do anything, Blue you need to feed. You're too weak," Surge told her. Tim and I nodded in agreement.

"Okay, fine go grab me a pouch from the truck, what's the big deal?" Blue asked.

"You need fresh blood Blue," Surge told her while placing a hand on her shoulder. She shook him off, as she sat and began to think. Drinking directly from a human was not ideal for her. Most vampires, once they turn on that kind of switch it's hard to go back to the pouches. Then life becomes more of a never-ending hunt than an actual functioning life.

"You got this Blue, you have so much self-control," Surge continued.

"Fine. But I certainly don't need an audience."

"Fine. Well, we will begin setting up camp. I know you can handle yourself," Surge told her. We gave each other a look as she began slowly walking towards the forest. It was unspoken but clear as day that I would keep tabs on her without her knowing. The last thing we need was for her to become rogue or lose herself in the hunt.

BLUE CHAPTER 37

"What are you doing!" I asked as I glared at Tristan before walking towards him. I could feel the anger rolling through me.

"Snap out if it Blue. Now." Tristan told me standing in front of me not backing down at all. He gently placed a hand on my shoulder and I started to rationalize. I felt as though I almost lost myself in the taste of the blood. I would've killed the human if Tristan didn't put two fingers into my wound. This is why when I regained self-control after being turned, I vowed to never drink directly from humans again.

The hunt was so intoxicating. I can still feel her warm blood pumping through my veins. It was delicious, no denying that. I can feel my eyes dilating and retracting, catching even the smallest movement, the smallest creatures on the fourth floor. The blood had me feeling supercharged. I cannot stand anything that makes me lose control like that. To not be in control of a situation is weak. I looked around the campfire as Tristan was gently pulling me from the forest. We were camping out near the cliff. Being so well prepared, we kept small tents and sleeping bags in all the SWE vehicles. Everyone was in their tents no doubt resting up for this inevitable mission we had to conquer.

"We will be resting here for a few hours then we will be hitting the road. We are only a few hours away," Tristan told me, then he walked both of us over to his tent. I didn't really feel like resting, let alone with Tristan but I knew it was what I needed so I didn't protest.

I woke up alone to the sound of Surge arguing with Micah. I came out of my tent and witnessed Tristan trying to keep my top two guards from ripping each other apart. My wound felt achy but I was in much better shape today than I was yesterday.

"She's going to kill you. Blue gave you a direct order and you straight up did what you wanted. This ain't no gang Micah." Surge was very upset. I took several deep breaths as I approached the guys. Tim also was woken up by the commotion and was walking up beside me.

"I need to be a part of this! It started with us three and it's going to end with us three!" Screamed Micah. I inadvertently felt the air around me. I felt the tension, stress, anxiousness, and above all else love. I also felt some familiar energy coming from the SUV Micah arrived in. Reece was here.

"Who's watching the Roses? If word gets out that we are all away on this mission and left the Roses unattended we will get taken over! Everything we fought so hard for will be gone! Don't you see that?" Surge was very distraught. He punched the SUV closest to him causing Reece to scream. Next thing I knew Micah had gotten around Tristan and punched Surge hard in the face using lightning-fast speed.

"You know that's where I draw the line Surge, never touch my old lady," Screamed Micah. They were in a full out brawl. I glared over at Reece. She stared back defiantly; I rolled my eyes. She knew better than to defy a direct order from me. On the other hand she wouldn't be my best friend if she did not have balls.

"Enough!" I held up my hand. I didn't scream but everyone stopped immediately. Reece jumped out the truck with her first aid kit. I knew now wasn't the time to fight with her.

"We are about to face something far worse than King. This squabble ends here and now. We need each other if we want to defeat the crazy humans, and save the white witch. Tristan, you have a plan?" I asked looking at him. I pretended not to notice Reece and Micah smirk at each other.

"I wouldn't be me if I didn't." He pulled a map out of his back pockets as he winked at me. He splayed the map out across the hood of the SUV.

"Okay so we know the tunnels were the easiest way to get to the lair but it was compromised. Our best bet is to park here and take the rest of the journey on foot. This area here seems to be less guarded than any other spot."

"That sounds too easy," Surge said. Back to his normal placidity.

"Well actually, it's going to be very hard to get in. There's a fifty-foot waterfall we will have to clear to get inside." We all looked around at each other. No doubt the only person all of them were worried about was me.

"We got this guys," I told them. Truth was, even without my wound I wasn't sure if I could jump that high. But I had to make it work. We all started loading up the SUVs.

TRISTAN CHAPTER 38

I had the strangest dream last night, Blue was in it. It felt as real as the dream I had with her before. This time we were in a totally different land fighting giants. I kept trying not to think about it, but I was not very successful at it. Which was how I allowed Surge to get past me and get to Micah during their fight. *I have to focus* I told myself. I had two clans depending on me. I owed Camilla so much. If it wasn't for her connections and intel, I would have never learned about this weak spot in the human's lair.

"Do they always fight so much?" I asked Tim as we threw the last tent in the trunk.

"You'll get used to it," he said with a chuckle. I won't lie and say that it didn't feel great to be included. But I knew I had to get back to my own clan as soon as this one was all over. The Cali clan needed me. And there were more than enough leaders here already.

We traveled in the SUVs for about two hours. We were already in Colorado at this point. We parked the trucks and would finish the rest of the journey on foot. Blue looked much better so I tried hard not to be overly worried for her.

"Tim, you will stay here. The rest of us will go in together," Blue ordered.

"I think we should split into two groups. Tim where did you put the walkie talkies?" I asked. Reece handed them to me before Tim could even register what I asked. She was a really quick thinker.

"Okay, Surge you're with me. Reece, Micah, and Tristan you approach on the left," Blue told us. Blue hugged everyone quickly. She saved me for last. I knew she wasn't the emotional type so I was so annoyed at myself when I felt such huge emotions after inhaling her sweet scent during our embrace.

"Be safe," she told me and kissed me on the cheek. The kiss reminded me of how hard it was not to rub on that ass last night.

"Let's roll out!" I ordered before I turned into complete mush. Micah gave me a look but he started walking. Reece and Micah had their small guns out in hand. I decided my first weapon of choice would be my assault rifle. I watched Surge lead Blue in the opposite direction. *Keep her safe* I thought to myself. We arrived at the waterfall much faster than I expected. Micah leaped into a tree with amazing speed and agility. Then easily leaped over into the waterfall. I couldn't see anything for a while but suddenly a guy dressed in all white fell from the waterfall. And I looked up to see Micah grinning with his golds showing. He motioned for us to join him.

"Okay you go up next," I told Reece. She barely lifted her hands as she floated up to the waterfall. I definitely underestimated her. I jumped up into the tree and then leaped into the waterfall just as Micah had. Once I got through, I noticed there was a huge white steel door. Three guards were laying in front of it.

"Okay Micah, I see you," I told him.

"Nah that was all Reece. She's not to be played with," Micah said feeling proud. Reece just shrugged and threw her golden locs over her shoulder.

"You remember that," She said flirtatiously, looking at her husband. I wasn't sure how we would get through the door but I decided we would wait here for Blue and Surge.

BLUE CHAPTER 39

It was so hard for me to leap up into the waterfall. I almost lost my footing but Micah caught me just as I was about to fall off of the slippery rock.

"Thank you," I told him, not looking at him. I hated needing help.

"You're good," He replied. We all stood in a semi circle around the white steel door.

"So how are we going to get in?" Tristan asked.

"Stand back," Reece told everyone. She drew in a deep breath. As she exhaled, she pushed her palms out toward the door. In just two attempts the door was pushed off the hinges with such force. She didn't even break a sweat. She even took two more guards down by pulling their hearts right out of their bodies.

"Okay now I really understand y'all's friendship." I told the ladies.

We all smiled, and Reece giggled but the excitement only lasted for about three seconds because we were immediately surrounded by a dozen men wearing white protective armor.

Their guns were drawn out. I hope Tristan is as good in battle as he boasts, because my team was already used to having to be quick on their feet. I was in the middle of our semi circle with Surge on my right. Micah was on my left. I gave them a head nod and started shooting. They immediately covered me. I didn't miss not one guard that I aimed at. I'm not going to lie, there was no other feeling in the world than fighting besides these two. It was as if the time had slowed down as I was firing. The trust we had amongst the trio was unbelievable. I noticed Tristan taking Reece out into the hall. They could see we had this area covered.

"All clear," Surge rang out. The three of us went to join the other two. We walked through the area that we just cleared out and shot at a biometric fingerprint door lock. After three shots, it finally opened. As soon as it was opened, we noticed there were humans everywhere. Many were wearing some kind of lab coat, they clearly never expected us to make it past the front room. We didn't stop anyone from running away, but the ones coming at us were immediately annihilated. There were just so many of them. Surge ordered us all to pick a corner while he squatted behind a metal hospital bed. They started to come in one by one and they did not stand a chance. There was an unspoken understanding that we all were to take turns taking them out. It was working well until they all stopped coming in all of a sudden.

"Somethings not right!" I screamed out. I could feel it. Surge was a half of second too late in reaching the door before one of the guys dressed in white closed us in. We all stepped out from our corners. Green gas began to come through the vents making it difficult for all of us to breathe. Tristan and Reece seemed to be doing better than the rest of us. They both ran to the door and began shooting and using magic to try and break the biometric security lock. I felt my mind getting fuzzy and my body losing its strength. *Oh no* I thought as I passed out.

"Blue." The voice was familiar. *The white witch.*

"Where are we Ma'am?" I asked her, not sure of what to call her.

"Please call me Alexandria. We are in an unconscious state and it's allowing us to communicate. You need to end this!"

"What exactly is this? What do these people want? And how can humans take down vampires as strong as us?" I asked, feeling very uneasy about being in an unconscious state vs awake and fighting.

"This place was created for the sole purpose of research. They are trying to come up with a plan to kill all vampires off the earth," She said wearily. I gasped.

"That still doesn't explain how they are pulling all this off," I said

"Tabitha, Tristan's psychotic sister set all of this up."

"What? Why?" I asked.

"Jealousy is an ugly thing. She knew where the cold ones kept the vampire history books. She made a deal with the green group in exchange that they would keep her safe during the deaths and murders of all the other vampires," She explained. I stayed silent for a minute I had a hard time understanding why someone would let jealousy run their lives.

"We have to stop her."

"Yes, and we will but right now you need to wake up Blue."

TRISTAN CHAPTER 40

It was a miracle that I was still standing. The green fumes burned my nostrils and made my stomach hurt but I was doing so much better than my comrades over there on the floor. Suddenly the green smoke stopped coming from out of the vents. I sighed with relief. The green smoke was replaced with white smoke and Reece who was feeling fine up until now began to cough. She looked like she was about to pass out. I caught her on her way down. She grabbed my arm with the strength she had left.

"Save Blue, Tristan," was all she managed to croak out.

"I will," I told her firmly. After placing her on the ground gently, I quickly took my book bag off and grabbed a grenade out. Blue wasn't the only one with cool gadgets. I grabbed everyone up and moved them from the door using lightning speed and strength. I threw the grenadine at the steel door and huddled down on the ground in readiness for the explosion. I threw my body over Blue and the others. The bomb went off with a loud crack. After some of the smoke cleared, I went over to the door. But it didn't even make a dent.

"Damn!" I cursed out loud. I suddenly heard many footsteps coming. Before I could even react, around twenty guards dressed in all white had filled the room. A small framed guy walked in after, accompanied by Tabitha.

"Oh, little brother! You fell right in my trap," Tabitha sneered.

"What the hell are you talking about? Why are you here?" I asked. My gun still drawn.

"Ah ah ah," the small guy said shaking his finger side to side.

"You might not want to do that if you care about your little blue-eyed friend over there," He warned me. One of the guys in white had a gun pointed right at Blue. *Oh, I'm going to kill all of them.* I thought, seething. I dropped my gun feeling weaker in that moment than I ever had before. I looked at Surge's huge body lying limp on the ground. I knew he would be pissed. All of them would be. I hung my head low, unable to think of a plan to get us out of this.

"I'm in control of all of this Mr. Royal. I'm Dr. Ren. I find you people feel more comfortable when I approach you as an equal. But just so were clear right now I have the gas just strong enough to knock your friends out, but with a simple push of a button I can kill them." He told me standing a full foot or more below me. *How did he know I was a Royal?* I looked over at Tabitha.

"What do you want? Is all of this because you are so small, do you have little man syndrome?" I asked him genuinely curious. He was even smaller than Lolli.

"Oh wow did you just try and make a joke?" He asked me as he held out his gloved hands as one of his minions removed one of his gloves. His tiny hands were severely burned.

"Damn, put the gloves back on!" I told him.

"You see, this is the result of me pissing off a witch. As a mere human the pain she caused me was horrible but nothing compared to her taking away my prize possession." He couldn't take his eyes off of his horrible looking hands.

"I was the best surgeon to ever do it and now I couldn't perform surgery on a lab rat. People like you make me sick but I'm not an animal. I'm going to make sure you are all under anesthesia as I perform my experiments. Human tech and medicine has many advances but until we tap into what makes you all so great we can only get but so far." He had a horrible smile. *How could a doctor just let his teeth go like that? I'll figure this out* I thought.

I was hit in the head from behind as they began to drag us all out.

I woke up in a cell with Micah and Surge. They were already awake. Surge appeared to be scanning the surroundings, looking for any possible way out. Micah was screaming through the bars.

"Let me the fuck outta here! If y'all hurt Reece or Blue I'm going to kill y'all!" I had to tune him out so that I could focus on getting us out of this situation. A technique I actually learned from Blue. I looked at the bars, they were too strong to break. The lock was legit. The floors were cement, and the ceiling was cement too. This one was really going to be a challenge. Suddenly everything got warm the way it does when the white witch is approaching. To my surprise, it wasn't her. Instead, the face that emerged made me stand up off the bench I was sitting on.

"Tristan, don't worry. Reece and I are safe." The holographic Blue told me.

"How the hell are you even doing this?" I asked. I noticed Surge and Micah could see her too.

"We don't have much time. I'll explain later. But Reece is working on our lock now, as soon as we are free. She will be there to unlock you guys. Tristan, soon as you are free you need to get to the white witch. The rest of us will have to fight the bitch that locked us up in here." She looked at me.

"Your sister," She said grimly. I was unsure of how I felt about it. But I didn't have time to dwell. I just nodded.

Suddenly we heard Reece from a distance whisper,

"Blue I got it, let's go."

"Okay see you all in a sec," Blue told us as she disappeared. Reece came around the corner very stealth like, followed by Blue many seconds later. They were both wearing all black like the rest of us. It was really easy to notice the blood Blue had attempted to wipe from her mouth. I shook my head in worry as me and Surge caught each other's eyes. We both understood just how hard it is to knock human blood. It's very easily addictive. I was worried this would happen, but we did not have a choice. She must have killed a human on her way here and had a taste of his blood. The lock popping open snapped me back to focus. It was in that moment that I knew, it was meant for us five to be here and it reminded me of the stroll I read: *Five is opportune.* If that part of the stroll made sense to me then we should think about the rest of it, and get as many answers from it as we can.

"The witch is three rooms over," Blue told us with her eyes closed, hands open and fingers splayed by her side.

"I sense about ten vampires and five humans in between us. They are confident and heavily armed. Let's be careful and make this quick," She continued.

"Blue, I think I should lead this one. We need you get to the white witch by any means. Stay at my six." Surge gave everyone a solid glance and nod.

"Okay," Blue told him. She grabbed my hand and squeezed but we both let go immediately. I felt the tingle left behind from an electrifying shock, and noticed she was squeezing her hand as well. But we did not have time to discuss this as we were all moving forward, following Surge into the battle.

BLUE CHAPTER 41

We were all so focused on getting to the white witch, the vampires didn't stand a chance. We fought our way through them. And in the last room, Reece pulled a new trick out of her hat that allowed her to cast a spell which pulled the souls out of the enemies and burst them in mid-air. Tabitha however managed to slip through the door just in time to still survive.

"Why all the chicks Tristan know be crazy and trying to kill us?" Micah asked.

"Get your shit together before you try and get back with my sis." I just rolled my eyes, he must of heard about Crystal. Tristan ran after Tabitha before we could stop them. Okay, so my plan just flew out the window. Alexandria was not only in a cell but they also had her strung up by her arms and hooked up to some sort of machine. She looked ghastly. Torn rags were only covering her private areas. She was covered in burns, cuts and bruises. It was a horrible sight.

Can we just unplug this? Micah and Surge were covering the door. Shots rang out as vampires and humans alike were still coming at us. Reece and I walked around the large machine, looking for a way to disconnect it. Suddenly, Alexandria spoke in a hushed tone.

"You cannot unplug this machine or it will blow us all to pieces along with everyone in a hundred-mile radius. There's a small town nearby they are innocents." She explained.

"So, what do you propose? Because this ends today." I told her while gently pulling on the chains and ropes that Alexandria was attached to.

First things first, pull out your spell book. She told me telepathically.

My spell book? Wait how are we able to communicate like this? I placed a hand over my mouth. Shocked by all of this.

Use your mind Blue. You are a marvel like no other. You already have the answers.

I did not say anything for a second. But I pulled out my book that my dad had left me. I gently waved my hands over the pages and it went to the page that I needed on its own. I'm not sure how I even knew to do that. The spell I cast was in a foreign language. The rope and chains instantly fell to the ground. Alexandria floated down gently onto the bench. I noticed Reece in the corner of the room, clearly scared to get near the white witch.

"You're fine my child, under these circumstances, you're fine. It is not your time Reece," Alexandria whispered as she slumped over on the bench, clearly very weak.

"I don't understand any of this," I blurted out as I covered Alexandria in a large Black sweatshirt Surge tossed over to me.

"Your father was a warlock, but not just any warlock. He was a part of the witch council, which is equivalent to being a king or queen in witch society. One of our only rules as councilmen is to not get too close to humans." She suddenly looked down, which made me brace myself for the next part of her story.

"Your dad happened to be in Korea when he stumbled into a war. Your mother was there. He described it to me as love at first sight. Before he knew it, he interfered in the war. He saved your mother, and ultimately saved many people from your country. The vampire council, however, did not see this as a good thing. There has never been a witch-human child of such high witch power in our history, which is why your blood is craved by other vampires."

"My mom kept this secret from me all these years? Where is my father now?" I asked her. Trying to not get upset because the mission wasn't over yet.

"Your mom had no memory of your real father. I had to take her memories and yours as well." Alexander said as she looked me straight in my eyes.

"Your father's dying wish was for me to keep you and her safe. That was the only way I could do to ensure that. But right now, we have bigger issues. The machine has enough of my blood to follow through with the green group's plans." She suddenly did not look so good.

"They took too much of my blood. I'm much too weak to stop this."

"What can we do to stop this?" I asked her. I could feel the despair and worry coming from her.

"The machine is going to need some of *your* blood," She said through teary ears.

TRISTAN CHAPTER 42

I chased Tabitha and never let her out of my sight. Her hair looked like a dancing flame and was my focus point. I know she was probably shocked that I was able to keep up with her. Finally, she stopped because she had nowhere to go. We were on a ginormous cliff, up so high even a vampire wouldn't survive the fall. She had two guards with her.

"Kill him," She told the largest one. He nodded and begun to come at me.

He swung hard and fast, and even with my super speed I barely avoided such force. These guys were no joke, but neither was I. I jumped up and landed a crushing blow to his face and heard his jaw break. He was down. I finished it off with mercy. A quick shot to the head and he was done!

"I don't want to get involved in family affairs," said her second guard as he disappeared back towards the green group building.

"I'm going to kill him when I get back," Tabitha said rather confidently. She got into a fighting stance. I put my gun away, I was no longer outnumbered and I've always preferred fighting with my hands.

"I just have a question for you sister. Why did you reveal my lineage to me? What did you get out of that besides the pleasure of acting like you did not know me at the Vampire council meeting?" I asked her as we circled each other.

"Well dear brother, I wanted to have you distracted enough so that you wouldn't get involved. You are of royal blood remember? That means you are indeed a good challenge. Unfortunately, your love for Blue," she said as she rolled her eyes, "caused you to still become involved. So now I have to kill you," She said as she hissed.

"Damn. Why does everyone hate on my baby love?" I asked jokingly.

"Besides, your plan sucked and you are about to die," I said taking a swing and missing. Oh she's fast too!

"Not so fast dear brother. I'm far from stupid. The plan is still in action and you can't do anything to stop it. Why do you think I lured you out so far away?" She chortled. My heart dropped a little as I thought of Blue. *Please be strong Blue.* I thought to myself.

"What the hell is the plan and what do you get out of this?" I had to know before I killed her. She chuckled.

"Well just the end of all vampires of course. So we created a potion out of that witches blood. It has angelic properties in it that go against the very nature of our blood, so it's deadly to any of us. We are going to drop a bomb over the world containing the potion," She told me.

"So, you're on a suicide mission?" I asked her slightly confused.

"No silly. I will be the only vampire still around. I've invested millions in this project to do so. That way I can create my own race that are loyal and obedient to only myself. Do you know how frustrating it is to be queen of the vampires but no one even knows who you are, nor do they care that they just lost their King? Blue is the most popular vampire of us all. It's infuriating," She stammered.

"You lost your father and you're hurting I get that, but all this because you are jealous of Blue?" Women are crazy.

"You could never understand my pain. He may have created you but you don't *know* our father. As far as I'm concerned, Blue should have been killed but the green group is filled with too many imbeciles!" She shouted.

Suddenly I was hit with so much force I almost lost my footing. I regained it just in time. We were now in a real battle. I was going blow for blow with my sister, and she was spectacular I will give her that. But I knew I had to end it. I dodged one of her blows and grabbed her up from behind. I had her in a chokehold and she couldn't breathe.

"Please Tristan, brother I love you," She choked out.

"I love you too," I said as I snapped her neck. It really did hurt me to have to kill my own sister. I sat down on the ground for a second to process everything. Suddenly Blue's face appeared.

"Tristan, I know you are hurting. But I need you," Blue said. It's going to take me some time to get used to all of these new abilities she now has.

BLUE CHAPTER 43

After Alexandria informed me that my blood is the only thing that could save the people I cared about, I knew I had to do it.

"How do we know Blue will survive this? Not to be rude but you look horrible Miss. And Blue is new to all this having powers and shit," Micah said.

"You are right to worry Micah. The machine does require much strength and even if you were fully healed, it would require more than you can give," Alexandria told us all. Just as Tristan burst through the door. Tristan looked at Surge.

"Did you bring the scroll?" He asked him. Surge handed the scroll to him.

> When times are bad turn to the cerulean sea
> Think old days aquamarine
> What's hidden will be revealed
> Five is opportune
> Chase the hottest of fires
> Remember strength brings fear

> Fear brings the fight
> Hold hands during the last hour

The last sentence of the scroll suddenly spoke to me. I met Tristan's eyes. I knew what I had to do.

"Tristan, I think if we were to hold hands then I can do this," I said with confidence. Alexandria nodded so I held out my hand. When our fingers interlocked, our hands glowed.

"What the fuck?" Micah said as Surge and Reece shushed him.

"Okay Surge, hook the red wire up to Tristan and the Blue wire to Blue," Alexandria said.

"Well that's a bit on the head." Tristan said.

Surge helped Tristan while Reece helped me. Once the needle was in both of our arms Micah turned the dial on the machine in the opposite direction. At first, we felt nothing.

"I don't think it's..." I couldn't finish my sentence because it felt like I was instantly hit by lightning. It's was excruciating. Tristan was already hollering. I tried to hold my scream as long as I could but I too joined him. Surge was pacing, I knew he was worried about me.

"How much longer?" Micah asked. It felt like the pain lasted forever but then the machined burst into flames.

"It's done we must go," Said Alexandria. Surge grabbed the white witch and carried her in his arms. Reece threw an energy ball at the wall that broke through five super thick layers of cement and metal walls. We could now see the lush greenery from the woods outside surrounding the place.

"Impressive, Reece." Said Alexandria. Reece grinned wide in delight. Micah slapped her butt and said,

"Go bae." Reece blushed as she gave her husband a look of content. Micah and Reece began making their way out. Tristan and I disconnected the wires from our forearms and just stood there looking at each other. Majority of the room was on fire around us and I felt frozen in place, staring into the pools of caramel that were his eyes.

"Come on Blue," Surge commanded as he turned around and noticed me and Tristan were still inside.

"Right behind you," I yelled at Surge, never taking my eyes from Tristan. We had just completed the impossible, simply by holding hands.

"Why do you fight against our love so hard?" Tristan asked me, staring deep into my eyes. Why was I so mesmerized? I couldn't look away.

"This love thing weakens me," I said. Why was I talking like this? I looked down and we were still holding hands. I slowly slid my hands from his and instantly felt my head clear.

"It must be the connection making me feel so uncharacteristic, come on, this place is on fire let's go!" I told him. I began walking away but I knew he was still standing there.

"Come on Tristan I don't want to die here!" Why did I care? Why was I still standing here? I could just walk away, but yet, I couldn't.

"No. I'm not going anywhere until you kiss me. Blue, how can you deny a love that even haunts you in your dreams?" He asked staring at me so passionately. I knew with every fiber of my being that he loved me in a way that others prayed for.

"You are the love of my life. In this life and the next. Under this moon or another, I will always find you," Tristan told me. I gasped. I've heard that line before. In my dreams.

"Oh my!" I exclaimed. I hugged him tightly. I could no longer crush the feeling that always crept up into my soul whenever I was around this man.

"This love won't make you weak Blue. As you saw firsthand, this love strengthens you." He held me tight before letting up and kissing me eagerly.

BLUE CHAPTER 44

Once we arrived back in the city there were so many things running through my mind. The main thought though was of Tristan. The kiss had me wanting more and the success of the battle finally allowed me to let down my guard. The guys all met with Tim and drove back while Reece and I booked a flight. We giggled on the entire flight back home like teenage school girls. Why had I denied myself this feeling for so long? The least I could do was give it a chance. The best part of it all was I no longer felt that having a man would make me any less than what I am, if anything it will strengthen me.

I don't know how but Alexandria was standing in front the Roses when Reece and I were getting out of our Lyft. Reece quickly went inside.

"Catch you later Blue," She told me.

"Omg you look amazing. How is this possible?" I told her in disbelief. She looked just as she did when we first met, pristine, and beautiful.

"After being freed from that machine my powers came very quickly with the help of my sister witches. Blue you saved us all, now let me save you." She looked at me with soft eyes as she began to walk towards me.

"Okay, well come on up and I'll get some food delivered, wait do you eat food?" I asked her. She didn't respond, instead she placed her hand on my abdomen and I instantly felt the pain being sucked out of me and my wound healed almost instantly. *I'm always with you Blue,* she told me telepathically. And just like that she was gone. I felt amazing!

***

Once I was showered and rested I texted Tristan. *Are you still in Baltimore?* For the first time in my life I was giddy and completely wrapped up in a man. I'm not going to lie it feels amazing considering the fact that just months ago I was perfectly content with dying alone. Tristan's reply was somewhat instant: *You know I am. You wanna go out?* I responded *No I want you to come over.* He relied *OMW* with a smiley face.

I was covered minimally tonight. I had my braids pulled up into a pony tail. I knew my dark skin was stunning in my emerald green silk teddy with the matching duster robe. I lit candles around the penthouse and put on some nineties r&b. I told my security they could have the night off. I felt very confident in not only my own abilities to protect myself but also in Tristan's. He couldn't take his hands off me from the minute I opened the door.

After that night Tristan and I started going out almost every night together. I was really enjoying getting dressed up especially because his reactions were always genuinely astounded. We were enjoying spending time with each other in the various hookahs in Towson, the bars in Fells point, and taking walks by the harbor. We even made it rain in Norma jeans strip club one night. Tristan better be happy I'm not the jealous type.

We frequently visited some of the most finest establishments Baltimore had to offer. Though we don't need human food I still enjoy nibbling on it and just enjoying the experiences. Most nights were filled with Tristan and I going out on the town but tonight we stayed in. There was something I had been wanting to get off of my chest and tonight just felt like the right time to do so.

"Hey, I need to tell you something about myself and I'm not a hundred percent sure how you are going to take it," I told him.

"Okay I'm listening what's up?" He asked.

"Well first I want to say that I'm not perfect and I've made many mistakes but there is only one mistake that I'm very ashamed of." Tristan told the pretty EHS he was drinking from that we needed a minute to ourselves. She looked a little disappointed but quickly gave us the room. He grabbed my hands and looked me in my eyes.

"Blue you are mine and nothing you say or do will change it." He was so serious. I kind of liked when he got all possessive about me. I took a deep breathe. His energy calmed me.

"And besides," he continued, "You're still with me out here and I don't even half way know who I am these days."

"Okay, well when I was first turned no one could control me or Micah except Surge. Our bloodlust was just too strong. One night Surge stepped out and Micah and I decided we were tired of being prisoners. We threatened a warlock in the Roses to teleport us somewhere far away or we would kill him." Tristan was trying really hard to keep his face neutral but it was not working. I could tell he was a little shocked. I let go of his hands and walked over the window. I did not want to see his face when I told him what happened.

"We ended up in Russia." I help my head down in disgrace as I continued.

"Micah and I slaughtered hundreds of people that night. We almost drank ourselves to death. The clan had to work overtime to try and cover up what we did in just six hours. Countless lives taken that night. I can never forgive myself." All the pain I had been holding onto from that night just could no longer be contained. I cried in Tristan's arms and he just held me. After a while he finally broke the silence.

"I heard about that massacre but the cover up was done well because I never even heard a rumor that the USE clan was involved. Yes what happened was awful, but Blue it's also the reason why you Surge and Micah are the most powerful trio I've ever met. You all went through that and came out stronger."

"I looked up at him. How the hell are you this amazing?" I asked him.

"Let me show you." He said softly as he began to kiss me gently all over.

TRISTAN EPILOGUE CHAPTER 45

It's been three months since we shut down the green group. I had decided to stay here with Blue after everything went down to make sure she was really safe. I enjoyed just being around her. She finally began to let me in, slowly, but surely. There was a beautiful going home ceremony that Blue and Reece put together for Red as soon as the white witch had gained enough strength to relieve her of this world. Even Allegra made it. I know she had a soft spot for Red so I definitely wanted to be here and be that shoulder she could cry on or in Blue's case, simply lean on.

I know we are supposed to be the good guys, but sometimes you have to do what's best for you. I told myself as Lolli used his telepathy powers to control the minds of the guards in this D.C. museum. I snatched the blue aquamarine necklaces from the display case. Alarms started going off immediately but the guards barely even saw me run past them. These necklaces have belonged to Blue and I since the beginning of time. Surge and I did some research with the help of Reece and we discovered they also store our powers, kind of like a backup energy source if we ever were in a bind.

The Baltimore clan

That was a few weeks ago, now I knew it was time to return to the caves. Landing in Cali put a smile on my face, I absolutely loved the west coast. Once in the caves and after a shower, I decided I would pay Camilla a visit. She stopped responding to my texts and only reached out to me if it were really important. I knew she was upset and the fact that I no longer knew if I belonged in the Cali clan anymore is probably going to make everything worse.

Opening my door, it felt good to be back in my own space. The feeling actually did not last long though because I sensed someone was in here. I placed my duffle bag down silently and pulled my gun from its holster.

"Absolutely no need for that, I'm unarmed." Lolli said as he came out of my bathroom with the sly expression he always had.

"What the fuck are doing here Lolli, I could of killed you?" I asked him as I put my gun back in its holster.

"Well, kid we have a problem. Your sisters death brought about a lot of attention and after a lot of digging they found out where you are, and more importantly who you are." He told me leaning in my doorway.

"Damn do they know I killed her?" I asked him.

"Yes, because you left a loose end. This is why I told you playing hero is not worth it. It's why your mom isn't with us today!" His expression lost all its humor when he brought up my mom.

"I understand you don't get it. I love protecting people and I can take care of myself, just like I told you before. So you don't have to keep following behind and worrying," I told him.

"You are in over your head, you don't realize just how powerful the royals are. I'm staying close to you whether you like it or not. Your mother is the only reason I'm here."

"Look I don't have time for this. I need to shower and head over to Camilla's." I ended the conversation as I made my way to my bedroom. *I know this motherfucker ain't been wearing my shoes!* I thought to myself noticing my shoes had been slightly rearranged. I decided I would ask Lolli about that another time. Even though Lolli thought he was my god dad he felt more like a brother to me and I'd hate to have to whoop his ass over my shoes.

Camille answered her own door once I arrived at her crib and I instantly knew something was up.

"Where's all the guys?" I asked her.

"I told them I needed a hour alone, so that we could talk." She said quietly. It made me nervous because last time she sat me down like this it was to tell me she wanted us to be together. I really hope this is was not about anything like that.

"Um, okay I'm listening" I told her.

The Baltimore clan

"Okay so first I need you to promise you won't explode."

"I won't explode, now what's up?" I asked her getting impatient.

"My dad wasn't the good guy many people thought him to be. In fact my dad was very much obsessed with power." She informed me.

"Okay well no one is perfect."

"I'm going to just spit it out. My dad knew you were from the Royal clan. When you came to us when you were twenty two they paid my dad a lot of money to keep you here with us and to have you believe you were a turned vampire. You don't remember anything because I believe you have had your mind wiped twice." She said waiting for a reaction. I was actually having a hard time digesting it.

"Really? Well where did I grow up because according to my sister and Lolli I was taken away from mom at a very young age." I asked her suddenly hungry for some answers.

"I'm so sorry, I don't know but my first guess would be an human orphanage." She began to sob.

"Well you have nothing to be sorry about." I told her patting her back. The look she gave me said otherwise. I slowly removed my hand from her back.

"Wait how long have you known all this?" I asked her.

"Since you first arrived. I'm so sorry. My dad did not even want me to know but I did some snooping on my own." Her eyes were red and puffy.

"I trusted you Camilla. When your dad past away that was your moment to be honest with me. I don't belong here!" I was on my way to the door. She ran after me still crying.

"This is why I did not say anything. I knew I would lose you." Her voice breaking as she cried was too much. I turned around and held her as she cried. Camilla was a lot of things but she was my family no matter what, and this hurt. I hated that I had to leave her but I did not belong here anymore. I needed to find out more about my past in order to properly move forward. I'm not sure if I want to actually work at the Roses but I know everything will fall into place once I get my mind right.

Suddenly I got a whiff of Gucci bamboo, Blue's most worn fragrance. *I miss you Tristan, come back to me.* It was Blue sending me a telepathic message. We had the necklaces customized to our taste, neither of us touched the precious aquamarine though, because it was already perfect. Ever since we started wearing them, we found out we can communicate telepathically whenever we felt like it. And so far, no distance has affected our messages. *I'm on my way, my love.* Little did my chocolate bunny know that I may not know everything but I do know Blue is my person. I'm ready to put a ring on it! *First*

I'll need to talk with Surge. I thought to myself as I scrolled through my phone, eagerly searching for a first-class seat to the BWI airport. *Mrs. Smith has a ring to it, but Mrs. Royal sounds perfect!*

Stay on the lookout for more **Ebony Vampire Novels.**

Follow me on IG @ms._mayo

Made in the USA
Monee, IL
20 September 2021